BEWARE

Mr Browser's choir was becom... rest...

'Tell us what you want us to do,' pleaded Michael, 'so that we can do it and go back home.'

'I will tell you what we need you to do,' said the Prime Brain Sharpener, ignoring the part about going back home. 'What does a choir usually have to do?' he asked.

'Sing songs,' calls out Anna impatiently, thinking that the Brain Sharpeners were still playing about.

'That's exactly right,' went on the Prime Brain Sharpener. 'We want you to sing some songs. And now you had better go to your quarters for food and a sleep. You will enjoy the food here—we have pills to provide humans with all the vitamins they need.'

Also in Beaver by Philip Curtis

Mr Browser Meets the Burrowers
Mr Browser and the Mini-Meteorites
The Revenge of the Brain Sharpeners

BEWARE OF THE BRAIN SHARPENERS

Philip Curtis

Illustrated by Tony Ross

Beaver Books

A Beaver Book
Published by Arrow Books Limited
62–65 Chandos Place, London WC2N 4NW

An imprint of Century Hutchinson Ltd

London Melbourne Sydney Auckland
Johannesburg and agencies throughout
the world

First published by Andersen Press 1983
Beaver edition 1987

Printed and bound in Great Britain by
Anchor Brendon Ltd, Tiptree, Essex

ISBN 0 09 954080 0

Contents

1
The Kidnapped Choir

Spiky Jackson was putting the finishing touches to a group model of the Eiffel Tower when Mr Sage, the Headmaster, brought Mr Jolyon Morten, the Inspector, into Mr Browser's classroom to have a look around. Mr Morten smiled at Spiky and Mr Browser, looked at the model and asked one or two questions which no one could answer. Then, according to his habit, he shot a question on quite a different matter to Mr Sage, taking him by surprise.

'I've been thinking about the music in the school,' he said. 'You haven't had a school choir for some time, I believe?'

'We've had difficulties since Miss Hobday left,' admitted Mr Sage. 'We haven't had a music specialist since.'

'That's hardly necessary,' said the Inspector, showing his teeth in an aggressive smile. 'I'm sure you have one or two teachers who can play the piano.'

'Only Mr Browser,' said the Headmaster, 'and possibly Mr Caracco, though he concentrates on the guitar.'

'The guitar! Most interesting,' said Mr Morten.

'I'm sure that between you a choir could be formed. The Choir Festival has dwindled in size of late, and an entry from Chivvy Chase would be very welcome.'

'I'll see what can be done,' promised Mr Sage.

'I'm sure you'll manage it,' said the Inspector, directing his smile at Spiky and Mr Browser. He shook hands with Mr Sage and made off for lunch at his favourite school, and Mr Sage went to his study to think.

He thought for a couple of days, on and off, and then went straight to Mr Browser's classroom.

'I was thinking that it would be a good idea if we formed a school choir to sing at the District Choir Festival,' he began.

'Yes, it's a pity Miss Hobday left,' said Mr Browser.

'Oh, we don't need a specialist,' said Mr Sage. 'Sometimes they're more bother than they're worth. I'm sure that you could do it, George. You can play the kind of songs the children like singing, I'm sure.'

Spiky Jackson, sitting at the front for his sins, pricked up his ears.

'What about Mr Caracco?' asked Mr Browser. 'He's more musical than I am.'

'Maybe,' agreed Mr Sage. 'But I still like piano accompaniments best. Besides, Mr Caracco's very busy with the school football team.'

'I'm not very fond of singing competitions,' objected Mr Browser.

'Oh, don't worry about that. Just let them do their best. I'm sure you have some very good singers in your class. Most of the choir could come from there.'

'I'll think about it,' said Mr Browser.

'Good man,' said Mr Sage, and went back to his room much relieved.

Two days later Mr Browser broke the news to Class 8.

'I'm forming a school choir,' he told them, 'and as this is the top class, most of the choir will come from here. We shall be entering the District Festival in two months, so there will be plenty of work to be done. There will be two practices after school each week. I shall be holding voice tests later this week, but you'll all be able to join unless I find any absolute groaners.'

Most of Class 8 could sing reasonably well, and the doubts of Spiky and Michael Fairlie and a few others were set at rest when they were assured that choir practices would not interfere with sporting activities. After Mr Sage had hinted that there would be a choir outing at the end of term Mr Browser's choir was as good as formed.

After the first practices most members of the choir went home reasonably happy.

'Remember Miss Hobday? She used to make us sing the same line ten times over before she was happy, and then it sounded no better than the first time,' said Anna Cardwell. 'At least old Browser lets us sing whole songs, instead of cutting them into little bits and making nonsense of them!'

'Maybe we won't be as good as Miss Hobday's choirs,' said her friend Thelma, who was an earnest recorder player, 'but I suppose we'll enjoy it more.'

'And the boys won't mess about so much,' added Anna.

'I reckon it'll be bearable,' Spiky Jackson was admitting to Michael Fairlie. 'At least he's chosen some decent songs – they're not all about mermaids and baby dragons, like Miss Hobday used to choose.'

'And the practices don't go on too long,' observed Michael. 'My dad said that if the choir stopped me from going to the Chase Boys football practices, he wouldn't have let me join.'

'I wonder where we'll go for an outing,' pondered Spiky.

'Nowhere, if we come bottom on points at the Festival,' declared Michael. 'You can tell old Sage is set on us doing well, or he wouldn't have turned up to the auditions and the first practices.'

Mr Sage did, indeed, attend all the practices in the first two weeks, now and again demanding that

mouths be opened wider and occasionally annoying Mr Browser by interrupting in the middle of a song. On the Tuesday of the third week, however, he couldn't attend because he had to go to a meeting of Headmasters. It was a warm, sunny day and the doors of the hall were thrown wide open so that Mr Browser's singers had plenty of air. Chivvy Chase School was otherwise almost deserted, because there is plenty for children to do on a warm day when lessons are over. The lollipop lady at the crossing held up the traffic for the last time as the few remaining stragglers crossed the road.

Mr Browser's choir sang 'The Skye Boat Song' and Spiky Jackson took a quick look at his watch. It was half-past four, and he was due at Lee Franks' party at five o'clock. As Lee was in Mr Caracco's class and had a voice like a lion with toothache, he had easily been able to avoid being chosen for the choir. Spiky knew that the best part of Lee's party would be the first part, when there would be plentiful supplies of food and drink available, most of which would no doubt be gone by quarter past five. It would take Spiky a quarter of an hour, running and walking, to arrive at Lee's house, so he became a little restive when Mr Browser announced the singing of another song.

This was 'Strawberry Fair', a song included at the request of Mr Sage, who had insisted that the choir should sing one or two old songs. This is the kind of song which needs a great deal of polishing, and because he was not too happy at its inclusion, Mr Browser seemed determined all the more to achieve perfection with it. The time slipped by, and because the choir was becoming bored, the singing became ragged. Spiky looked at his watch again – twenty minutes to five.

'We must get this right before we go,' declared Mr Browser. 'Try the last line once again.'

They tried it once again, and it wasn't any better. A gust of wind from the open doors blew Mr

Browser's music on to the floor, and caused further delay. Spiky's hand shot up in the air.

'Well, Simon?'

'Please, Mr Browser, I've a party to go to, and it starts at five o'clock. How much longer shall we be?'

Mr Browser frowned as he rearranged his sheets of music.

'As I told you, Simon, we must get this right first. Just one more try –'

Maybe Mr Browser was at the point of weakening and allowing Spiky to go, but a piercing cry from Anna Cardwell drowned his words.

'Look, Mr Browser! Guns!'

Mr Browser looked up from his music and the choir turned to see Anna pointing to one of the open doors. In the doorway a figure dressed in white was standing, holding a white shape which resembled a gun. Two other figures appeared at another doorway, and one leaned in at a window. Another gust of warm wind blew Mr Browser's music on to the floor again, but now he was no longer concerned about it. He rose to his feet.

'What do you want?' he demanded, thinking the figures might be something to do with a charity appeal.

'Don't shoot!' shouted Anna, as the gun shapes were raised. The figures pressed down a catch at the side of their guns, and Spiky felt a chill go through him. The whole choir shivered. The figures, wearing close fitting white jackets and trousers, had white hoods over their heads with gauze-like masks over their faces. No part of their bodies could be seen.

Strangely, as the icy wave hit them, the choir became conscious that they were being ordered to leave the hall. No word was spoken by the figures, but the message became clear in each person's mind – including Mr Browser's:

'Go to the school field.'

Spiky Jackson voiced the lingering remains of a protest.

'But I've a party to go to. It starts at five o'clock,' he tried to say in a voice which was feeble at the start and trailed off to nothing at the end. The figures ignored him, but used their weapons to threaten the children and move them on quickly. Mr Browser was still mentally fighting.

'You can't do this!' he declared in a voice which sounded like a hoarse whisper, although he thought he was shouting.

One of the figures pressed the catch on his gun again, and the perspiration on Mr Browser's forehead froze. He said no more – his mind and body had been numbed.

The figures guided the choir out of the hall and along a path towards the field. At this point a cleaning lady who had been busy in one of the

outbuildings, came out with a bucket in order to fetch some water from the main school.

''Ere – what's all this?' she demanded when she saw the silent procession.

In answer, the figures turned towards her and pointed their weapons at her. She literally froze as she stood there, a protesting look on her face. She fell like a block of ice on the grass by the path, and lay there in numbed silence.

On the field a strange object was shimmering. It was almost transparent, and resembled more than anything the effect which forms in the air at times of great heat. But there was no mistaking the shape: the thing looked like a giant pepperpot. The shock of this overcame the choir's numbness for a moment.

'It's them!' whispered Anna Cardwell. 'It's the Brain Sharpeners come back!'

'I had a feeling they might,' said Martin Portland-Smythe gloomily. 'But why, I don't understand. I thought they'd decided we weren't worth the trouble.'

The Brain Sharpeners, first alerted by Mr Browser's accidental use of their name in class, had already made two attempts to use Class 8 in an experiment to sharpen the brains of human children in order to colonise a new planet; once they had been foiled by Michael Fairlie, the second time by hostile tribesmen who helped Mr Browser and Spiky to scare them off.

'Can't we let somebody know we're going?' asked Anna. 'Please can't we let our mums know?'

The hooded figures took no notice at all of the feeble pleadings of several of the children; no one else was about on the school field, and soon they were being herded into the transparent pepperpot which the Brain Sharpeners had clearly devised in order to be able to make a daytime appearance without arousing suspicion.

Away on the road which ran beside Chivvy Chase

School, one or two passers-by became idly curious about the strange behaviour of some children on the school field. These children appeared to be going up an invisible spiral staircase and sitting on the steps of it, as if suspended in space. An old pensioner carrying a shopping bag rubbed his eyes and spoke to a woman passing in the other direction.

'Look at them kids,' he said. 'Who knows what they'll be getting up to next! It's some sort of gymnastic display, I suppose.'

'If you ask me, it's a waste of time,' observed the woman. 'They'd be better off at home doing some homework.'

The old man was not a hundred per cent sure that this was some kind of modern educational activity.

'There doesn't seem to be anything holding them up,' he said. 'If only I had my binoculars with me – my eyes aren't so good these days.'

A puff of dusty smoke or smoky dust came from the centre of the field, and when it cleared there was nothing to be seen of any children at all.

'Must've been dreaming,' mused the old man, and the woman hurried off quickly in order to avoid more conversation with such an odd fellow. Meanwhile, the only person who might have acted as a reliable witness to the flight of the choir, Mr Watchett the caretaker, was fully employed in

trying to bring round one of his cleaners, Mrs Harrison, whom he had found lying in a pool of water on the path, shivering as if she had caught a cold. Mr Watchett took her to the hall and sat her on a chair.

'Whatever happened to you?' he asked her when she had stopped shivering.

But Doris Harrison could make little sense of what had happened to her.

'I was walking along with me bucket in me hand,' she said, 'and suddenly I went all stiff. Then I must have fallen down, and I don't know any more until you came along.'

'You're wet through,' said Mr Watchett. 'I'll get my wife to bring across a blanket and some dry clothes – then you'd better go home and take it easy. Better call the doctor, too.'

'Don't bother – I'll be all right,' declared Doris, relieved to feel the blood flowing in her veins again.

'By the way,' said Mr Watchett, 'Mr Browser's choir must have packed up, I suppose? I didn't see any of them going home.'

'Can't remember seeing them,' said Doris, and she spoke the truth, for her not-so-sprightly brain had been totally numbed by the Brain Sharpeners at the same moment as they had frozen her body.

'You shouldn't rush about so much, Doris,' Mr Watchett advised her, and, taking his own advice, set about his duties at a steady pace. It was nearly half-past five, just as he was about to close the front door of the school and make for home in time for the news on T.V., when he was disturbed again, this time by the telephone. The caller was Mrs Jordan, mother of Selwyn in Mr Browser's class.

'Selwyn's not arrived home yet,' she informed him. 'Could you tell me when Mr Browser's choir left school? Surely the practice can't have gone on this long?'

'The choir's been gone a long time,' replied Mr Watchett, recalling that he hadn't seen them go. 'I expect they've been playing about on the way home. There's no knowing what the children of this school may be getting up to,' he concluded, under his breath.

'It's not like Selwyn,' said Mrs Jordan uneasily, for she knew from experience that if Selwyn were late, then something unusual must have happened. She thanked Mr Watchett and rang off. Her call was closely followed by others from Mrs Portland-Smythe, Mrs Fairlie and Mrs Cardwell, and Mr Watchett's patience became exhausted.

'Kids!' he muttered after he had slammed the receiver down on Mrs Cardwell. He almost ran to the door, locked it and made off down the path with the fear of a phone call hovering about his ears.

At the party, Lee Franks persuaded his mum to

wait for ten minutes before the attack on the food began, because Spiky was still missing, and Lee wanted to be well in with Spiky because they both played in the football team.

'Don't understand it,' he said. 'Spiky wouldn't miss the food bit if he could help it, and the choir can't have gone on so long. Hope he hasn't had an accident.'

He would have held out longer on behalf of his friend, but his dad came in, having left work specially early in order to be present at the feast.

'Wot's all this?' demanded Franks Senior. 'All sitting about in front of a loaded table, doing nothing? Waiting for me, perhaps?'

'No, Dad, we're waiting for Spiky,' Lee informed him. Mr Franks regarded Spiky as a possible rival to Lee at football, so he wasn't very sympathetic.

'If Spiky can't be on time, then he doesn't deserve anything!' he observed. 'Let's get cracking, and if there's anything left for latecomers, they're welcome to it!'

To show his goodwill he put his fist into a bowl of crisps and crunched away at them happily. Lee could now hold out no longer, for his mum always obeyed his dad instantly, and she was already serving out tasty morsels to the eager gathering. Lee spent a few seconds puzzling over the non-arrival of Spiky, then decided he would be foolish not to enjoy his own party, and forgot about him.

Elsewhere concern about the missing children was growing, and when Mr Portland-Smythe arrived home from his office he quickly proved that he was a man of action, even if he was no longer Chairman of the Parents' Association.

'Martin's not home from the choir practice yet,' said his wife, 'and I've rung up several other parents, and their children haven't come home either.'

'Have you rung the school?'

'Yes, of course. They're not there.'

'Who told you?'

'The caretaker, Mr Watchett.'

'I'll ring again,' declared Mr Portland-Smythe. He did, but he received no reply, as by now Mr Watchett was at home watching the news.

'Sage should know about this,' decided Martin's father angrily. 'I want to know at what time exactly the choir left for home. If he doesn't know, he'll have to ring Mr Browser to find out.'

Before he could lift the receiver the phone rang again. This time it was Thelma's mother, tearfully stating that she was ringing from a booth near the school, which was shut. There wasn't a child in sight.

'Don't worry,' said Mr Portland-Smythe threateningly. 'I'm just going to ring the

Headmaster, and we'll come up to the school and meet you there. He'll have to do something about it.'

'I can't understand it,' said Mr Sage when he was called away from his evening meal. 'Browser usually finishes by quarter to five. Surely Mr Watchett can't have locked them in? I'll be at the school within ten minutes.'

When he arrived at the school twenty parents of the thirty strong choir were already at the door discussing the situation excitedly.

'Strange things have been going on at this school,' Mrs Cardwell was saying. 'Once or twice I've thought of taking Anna away, and this could be the last straw.'

'I'm sure there must be some explanation,' said Mr Sage as he unlocked the door. 'Mr Browser is a completely trustworthy teacher, and I can't believe the children can have come to any harm.'

'Then where are they?' demanded Mrs Cardwell heatedly.

'We'll search the school,' said Mr Sage. 'It's just possible they're locked up somewhere. Children sometimes play about. Please go ahead and search, while I ring Mr Watchett.'

So the caretaker was recalled, and the school was searched hastily but thoroughly by the tense parents. Not one child was found. Mr Watchett shrugged his shoulders as much as to say, 'I could have told you so.'

'What now?' demanded Mr Portland-Smythe.

'Well,' said Mr Sage, 'as they're not on the premises, there isn't much more I can do about it – '

'Yes you can! Mr Browser is your teacher, and it's your choir. You're responsible for keeping them in after school!' shouted Mrs Cardwell.

'Please calm down,' pleaded Mr Portland-Smythe. 'Perhaps we should ring Mr Browser's home,' he suggested. 'If he's there, he can tell us when the children left school, and we shall know that they're up to something on their own account.'

Mr Sage frowned, but he went and found Mr Browser's telephone number, and the parents waited silently while he dialled the number. The conversation was brief, and Mr Sage looked even more serious when he put the receiver down than when he had lifted it.

'Mrs Browser can't help us,' he announced. 'She told me that her husband hasn't come home yet. She's very puzzled about it.'

'That man! He's gone off with the whole choir!' said Mrs Cardwell, sniffling into her handkerchief. 'I knew something dreadful would happen at this school.'

'Now now,' Mr Portland-Smythe calmed her. 'I'm sure the children will come to no harm if they're with Mr Browser.'

'Of course not,' agreed Mr Sage hopefully.

'But,' added Martin's father solemnly, 'at this stage, whatever has happened, I think it is our duty to inform the police.'

'Hear, hear!' said Mrs Cardwell.

'The police?' Mr Sage shrank from the publicity which might follow. 'Shouldn't we first make a search ourselves?'

'Where?' demanded Mrs Jordan. 'I've been up and down most of the streets round here. I agree. The police must be informed!'

The parents looked so fierce that Mr Sage knew that no other course was open to him. The Sergeant on duty at the Chivvy Chase Police Station then received the oddest phone call he had ever recorded.

'Can I help you?' he asked.

'Yes,' came a troubled voice. 'I want to report a missing choir.'

'Missing what?'

'Missing choir, with their teacher. Chivvy Chase School Choir is missing, and Mr Browser with the children.'

'You must be joking – who's that speaking?'

'I am the Headmaster, and I am by no means joking. I have a group of worried parents waiting here, all concerned about their missing children.'

'Hold on,' said the policeman. 'I'd better take

details, and I'll send someone round as soon as possible.'

With the rest of his staff around him, he wrote down all the particulars Mr Sage could provide. By the time he put the phone down, Chivvy Chase was the most puzzled police station in Britain. As for Mr Sage, he hoped the children were safe, and he dreaded the thought of what he might have to face in the future. What a feast the newspapers and even the T.V. would have when the news spread around!

If only he had never formed the choir, he thought. It was Mr Jolyon Morten, the Inspector, who was to blame, he reflected. But he quickly realised that he couldn't start blaming an Inspector. Oh dear, whatever had that wretched Mr Browser done with the choir! He stared hopelessly at the assembled parents, and they stared back at him.

That was how the police found them some minutes later.

2
On a Platform in Space

As soon as the members of the choir were all seated in the transparent pepperpot, the machine created its own cover by sending out a cloud of smoke and raising the dust all around it. When they emerged above this, the children were granted a brief view of the little world of Chivvy Chase beneath them. At the same time their stiffness and the numbness of their brains lessened, and they began to appreciate to the full what was happening to them.

'The Brain Sharpeners won't let us escape this time,' said Spiky, frowning.

Anna Cardwell looked down on the church and on Chivvy Chase School, and her round face puckered up and the tears began to flow freely.

'We'll never see home again,' she sobbed. 'Why do they have to come for us? Mr Browser, can't you stop them? I want to go home.'

'Yes, we want to go home!' pleaded a number of other voices.

'Are we going away for ever?' cried out Michael Fairlie to one of the figures standing below them, but the figures took no notice, only taking off their hoods and revealing the sharp features, large heads and piercing eyes of Brain Sharpeners.

'I wish I could jump through the side of this thing,' said Mark Austin. 'I'd rather die on Earth than – '

'Be quiet!' came Mr Browser's voice. Up to that moment he had been too stunned to speak, for the Brain Sharpeners had made quite sure that he, as leader, was powerless. Now that he was regaining his faculties, though he was horrified by the situation, he decided that he would have to try to behave like the teacher in charge of any normal school outing.

'The best thing we can do,' he said, 'is to keep calm and hope that maybe we are only going away for a short while. After all, Mr Salt came back after they had taken him – '

'And what a state he was in!' called out Anna.

'I can't see out any more!' said Martin. 'Something's happening to the outside of this – this machine. You can't see through it any more!'

The choir watched in silence as the pepperpot, like a chameleon, appeared to have changed its own colour. The distant earth was no longer visible as the craft lost its transparency and adopted a dull white colour, similar to the first craft which had appeared to Michael Fairlie. The construction of the molecules of the pepperpot was being changed, and soon the choir was enclosed in a world of its own.

'I wish I'd tried to jump!' declared Mark.

'You couldn't have done,' Spiky informed him. 'We're all locked in. If you lean forward, you'll feel a kind of bar across the front of you. Look – it's becoming visible, too!'

Each child was indeed encased by a solid bar, rather like the bars which protect skiers when they are on a ski-lift in the mountains.

'I wouldn't advise trying to jump out, even if it were possible,' said Mr Browser. 'We must be thousands of miles up in space by now. I repeat, keep calm and hope that we have been taken for some reason just for a while, and that after we have done what they want of us, we shall be allowed to go home again.'

His words were greeted with silence, as each one thought over the chances of persuading the Brain Sharpeners to let them return – and decided that they were very, very small indeed!

One of the figures below moved to the centre of the craft and operated several switches set into a long control centre. Beside each traveller there appeared a container shaped like a glass, full of colourless liquid. Alongside it was a blue pill about the size of a 5p piece. Simultaneously a large screen appeared high up in the centre of the craft, and this slowly turned so that all the passengers could read what was on it.

'All passengers,' read Spiky aloud, 'must drink and swallow the pill. The drink will help to stabilise the human body in space, and adjust it to the different gravity, and the pill will prevent you needing food during the twelve Earth hours of your journey. Failure to obey this order could mean possible collapse and even death.'

'Suppose it's some kind of drug?' queried Anna – but like the rest, she swallowed the pill and drank off the liquid in order to be on the safe side.

When he was sure that nothing was left, the figure beneath them pressed the switches again and the containers disappeared.

'Twelve hours' journey,' pondered Michael. 'We can't be going all that far – '

'All that far! You must be joking!' objected Selwyn Jordan. 'We can't tell how fast we are travelling, for one thing.'

'I mean,' said Michael patiently, 'it looks as though we're staying in our galaxy, not travelling on to some other galaxy where the Brain Sharpeners' world must be. We could be going to their Outer Space Station, which they've been using to look at the world – '

'That's far enough!' declared Anna. 'We could be travelling at ten thousand miles an hour – multiply that by twelve and I make it a hundred and twenty thousand miles we shall have gone. That's enough for me!'

And overcome by the size of her own sum, she burst into tears again.

'The only thing we can do is to wait and see what happens when we arrive,' said Mr Browser. 'If it takes us twelve hours to reach our destination, then it will only take us twelve hours to come back.'

This announcement was received with about as much enthusiasm as men adrift at sea would give to the suggestion that one day the wind might change direction.

'It's boring sitting here,' said Spiky, to change the subject. 'Have we got to look at each other and the walls for another eleven hours? I'm fed up already!'

As if they had listened to him, the Brain Sharpeners down below again became busy with their switches, and soon the large screen appeared again. On it there flashed a succession of intricate patterns, and then the first of a series of competitions played by two players. These consisted of highly advanced mazes and games of the Space Invaders type, and they were played between an oblong and a circle.

Under the influence of the screen, the choir became more relaxed, but the worries of Mr Browser increased. What could the Brain Sharpeners be wanting with this helpless group of children? Had they gone back on their decision not to use them for colonising one of their planets?

As the pepperpot spacecraft sped on silently through space, and the entertainment provided by the Brain Sharpeners flashed continuously on the big screen, the audience became drowsy and heads began to droop. The kind of amusement provided by the Brain Sharpeners, as might be expected, required concentration in order that it could be properly enjoyed, and the human brains found it more and more difficult to focus their eyes or their minds on the screen. One by one they dropped off into an uneasy sleep, and Mr Browser soon followed their example. Observing that their efforts were being ignored, the figures down below switched off the screen, and the passengers were left to doze through the remaining weary hours of their flight.

Half-an-hour before touchdown they were all wakened by a high pitched buzzing, the screen reappeared and the face of a Brain Sharpener was shown on it. He looked very stern and important, and the two figures below were just as attentive to him as were Mr Browser and his choir.

'I recognise him!' called out Michael Fairlie. 'He's the Commander of the Brain Sharpeners in Outer Space – I've met him before!'

'You are absolutely right, my boy,' said the stern

figure. 'You are all on your way to the Outer Space Station, where you will be told of our purpose for you.'

'Are you going to let us go back home again?' called out Anna, but in reply the Commander only frowned and then vanished from the screen. His image was replaced by an instruction written in capital letters: NO QUESTIONS MAY BE ASKED UNLESS PERMISSION HAS BEEN GRANTED.

This notice then also disappeared, and the figures below disposed of the screen again. There was no indication of the arrival of the pepperpot at its destination until a door in its side opened and a garish light flooded in, turning the children's faces a yellowish colour.

'We're here!' said Spiky. 'I'm not locked in any more.'

His companions discovered that the bars which had been across the front of them had vanished. The figures below indicated that they should lead out of the pepperpot. Mr Browser's heart began beating faster. Soon, he realised, they would learn how they were going to be treated.

'I've been here before,' said Michael as they filed out of the pepperpot and into a huge enclosed platform which reminded Spiky slightly of an exhibition building he had been to at Earls Court in

London, it was so huge.

'The floor moves in here,' Michael informed the rest.'You don't have to walk anywhere.'

But he was at once proved wrong. They were herded from the pepperpot into a large room at the side of the hall, where they were guided into seats which were arranged in tiers facing a huge, built-in screen. They were too overawed to do more than whisper, but after a minute or two their Brain Sharpener guides quietened them with imperious movements of their arms.

'Look!' whispered Michael, risking the wrath of the Brain Sharpeners. 'There's someone coming in on the moving floor I told you about!'

Michael had made a brief visit to the Outer Space Station previously, but the experience had been wiped from his brain until the reappearance of the Brain Sharpeners, so his friends stared at him disbelievingly when he claimed to be familiar with the place. In any case they were watching spellbound as the imposing figure of the Commander of the Outer Space Station was carried into the room as if he were on a moving walkway for passengers carrying heavy luggage. This walkway, however, was much more advanced than anything on Earth; the Commander only had to indicate with his claw-like hand the direction in which he wished to move, and the floor obeyed. It even took him up a little slope and put him on a slightly raised platform in front of the assembled children.

'Children of the Earth,' he addressed them in thin, accurate tones and perfect English. 'You are wanting to ask questions about your journey here. It is good that you use your brains to ask questions, and since on two occasions we decided to let you go, we can understand your curiosity about the reason for your journey.'

'That's cheek!' whispered Anna Cardwell so quietly that only Spiky next to her could hear her. 'We escaped from them, didn't we?'

The Commander paused and looked sternly in her direction, as though he had read her thoughts.

'The truth is that we decided that the brains of human beings are hardly worth pursuing, and the search for beings more suitable for the development of our colonies goes on elsewhere. The danger of humans becoming too aggressive, of mutiny and of strikes persuaded our leaders to call off the attempt to recruit young people from Earth to develop other worlds. Somewhere or other we are bound to find a more advanced civilisation, where we shan't have to work so hard on the people's brains. In fact, I was on the point of obeying instructions to remove this Outer Space Station to a more favourable position for further searches, when something happened which changed the whole situation.'

The large inbuilt screen behind the Commander began to flicker, and without turning to look at it the Commander spoke quickly and then stood to one side.

'My leaders are sending us a message – please listen carefully,' he said.

The flickerings on the screen gradually formed into the shapes of five figures seated at a horseshoe shaped desk. They were clearly beings similar to the Commander and the other Brain Sharpeners, but their heads were even larger and their features even sharper than the Commander's. While the Commander's head was supported by a sort of triple collar, with three spiky points on either side of his head, these Super Brain Sharpeners needed collars with four spiky points, which were in rich, velvet colours as opposed to the Commander's plain white – and the Prime Brain Sharpener in the middle had five points each side! The children were now in the presence of five Super Top Brain Sharpeners, whose eyes were more piercing than those of the Commander or of Miss Toms the Deputy Headmistress of Chivvy Chase School.

The Brain Sharpener in the middle addressed himself first to the Commander.

'We Brain Sharpeners have a responsibility to the Truth,' he said severely.

'I have been telling the truth,' protested the

Commander.

'Not the Absolute Truth,' insisted the Prime Brain Sharpener, as he was called. 'You children of Earth have caused us more trouble than we expected, and we have had to change our views on the nature of human beings as a whole. Our Outer Space Station has failed twice in reaching its objective – '

The Space Commander looked as wretched as a criticised Brain Sharpener can.

'We misunderstood the nature of the human brain. It is technically very advanced, but has not enough control over the emotions of humans. This led our Commander to underestimate what you humans call your "will" or your "spirit". Do you understand this, human children? Your people are clever, yet they are often not grown up. They will still fight instead of deciding problems by reasoning. They prefer to live in their own ignorance rather than allow themselves to be improved by a superior race such as ourselves. Those who understand, raise your right hands.'

The human children all obeyed to show that they understood, though, alas, about a quarter of them put up their left hands rather than their right.

'Good,' said the Prime Brain Sharpener. 'So because of this childishness, we instructed our Commander to waste no more time, but to prepare to remove the Space Station from your galaxy. Now, Commander, you may tell them what happened to make you change your mind.'

The Commander bowed to the images, which remained watchfully present while he took up the story.

'Accordingly,' he said slowly – clearly he was very much aware of the presence of his superiors on the screen – 'I set in motion arrangements to withdraw the Outer Space Station from the region of the Earth.'

The Prime Brain Sharpener yawned, so the Commander speeded up a little.

'Everything was ready, and we were awaiting instructions as to where to go, when our automatic scanner reported the presence of an unknown body approaching us from Earth. Quick calculations made us fear that the object was making straight for us, perhaps homing in on us. We put out a protective atmospheric shield to deflect the object – we use this to avoid small meteorites which might hit us while in flight – and we employed our microscopic telescopes to examine the object as it passed. To our surprise our back checks on its course revealed that it had come from Earth. It sped past us, heading far out into space, and there appeared to be no reason for it to stop unless it collided with a planet – or perhaps it was intended

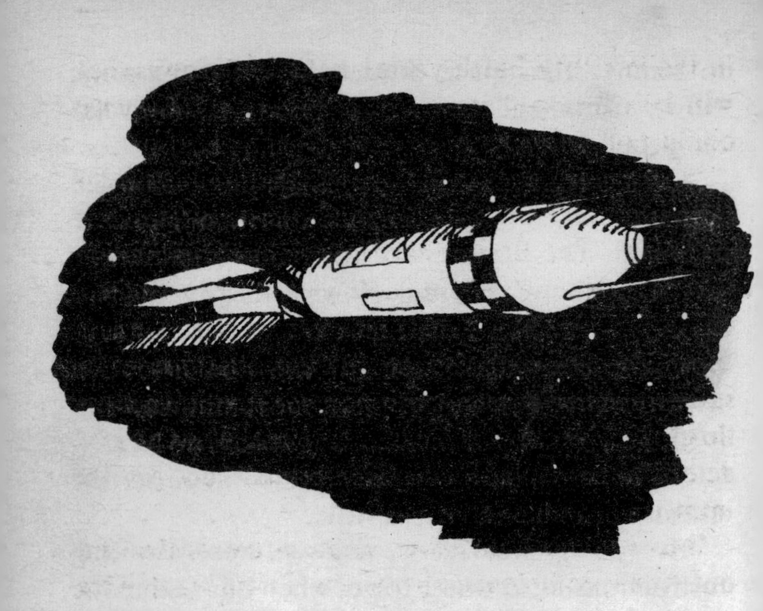

to collide with something? As it passed, we made our usual long range inspection which we carry out on any strange passing objects, and we were shocked to discover that in the nose of the rocket there was what you call a nuclear warhead, easily capable of destroying our Space Station, and perhaps even moving a small planet disastrously off course. Knowing the warlike nature of human beings, we felt it necessary to warn our own home base, though the likelihood of the rocket reaching there is very small.

'However, advances in science have been so vast

in the last fifty Earth years, that who knows what will be developed in the next fifty? So we felt we could not just ignore the matter.'

'It was probably an experimental rocket gone off course,' said Michael, nipping in with a quick comment. The Brain Sharpeners looked annoyed, but the Prime Brain Sharpener ignored the interruption.

'What the Commander has said is correct,' he said. 'We are following the progress of the rocket through space, and if it has been sent out to try and detect our home base, we shall destroy it immediately.'

'Most people don't even know you exist!' called out Anna, emboldened by Michael's outburst. This annoyed the Brain Sharpeners much more.

'Make sure these children do not interrupt!' the Prime Brain Sharpener demanded of the Commander, and he sent one of the guardian Brain Sharpeners to remove Anna and sit her in a vacant place near to himself. 'Since then,' went on the Prime Brain Sharpener, 'we have conducted a secret inquiry into the nature of weapons being created at the moment on Earth. To put it bluntly, we are appalled!'

'Our choir can't help that!' objected Michael, and to everyone's surprise, including the Commander's, the Super Top Brain Sharpeners all accepted this, nodding agreement between themselves.

'We understand that,' said the Prime Brain Sharpener. 'We also know that human beings value their children above all else – though there are a few exceptions who place animals first. We have decided that we must do something to teach human beings that the development of weapons of destruction is not a sign of civilisation, and could lead not only to the wiping out of the world but also could cause great danger to other civilisations such as ours, if the speed of invention continues as it has done. We have therefore decided to give the human race a warning – and we are going to use you to do it.'

'But why pick on us?' protested Spiky. 'Why not choose some other children for a change. There are plenty more, you know.'

The Prime Brain Sharpener smiled.

'The reason you were chosen concerns our Outer Space Station Commander,' he said, his rather mocking smile now directed at the Commander. 'We ordered him to obtain a choir of children for us, and because he had made two attempts to capture some of you, he must have felt inclined to try again. I believe on Earth you have a saying, "third time lucky", haven't you?'

'That's right,' said Anna, who was regaining her

confidence. The Commander tried hard to accept the words of his superior with dignity.

'I know the layout of Chivvy Chase School,' he declared in his own defence. 'That made it much easier for my helpers.'

Mr Browser's choir was becoming restless.

'Tell us what you want us to do,' pleaded Michael, 'so that we can do it and go back home.'

'I will tell you what we need you to do,' said the Prime Brain Sharpener, ignoring the part about going back home. 'What does a choir usually have to do?' he asked.

'Sing songs,' called out Anna impatiently, thinking that the Brain Sharpeners were still playing about.

'That's exactly right,' went on the Prime Brain Sharpener. 'We want you to sing some songs. And now you had better go to your quarters for food and a sleep. You will enjoy the food here – we have pills to provide humans with all the vitamins they need.'

'Pills!' said Spiky disgustedly. 'Are we going to have to live on pills?'

But the patience of the Super Top Brain Sharpeners was now exhausted, and they wanted no more discussion with mere Earth children. They faded quietly from the screen. The guardian Brain Sharpeners took over, and led the children and Mr Browser away to their quarters, which consisted of tiny bedrooms let into the walls of a long corridor. Spiky had seen something like it in a T.V. programme which showed pictures of a modern Japanese overnight hotel.

'What do they think we are – battery hens?' asked Anna, but nobody answered her. They had to file past the guardian Brain Sharpeners and receive two pills each, one red and one yellow. Some of the choir hesitated to swallow them.

'Food and drink,' said one of the Brain Sharpeners.

'Better take them,' said Mr Browser, 'and try to have a good night's sleep.'

But was it day or night? The confused members of the choir had no idea; they took their pills and went to their sleeping quarters, each one alone.

'Sleep well,' came a voice from the wall in each compartment. 'You will be awakened by me in eight Earth hours' time, when you will begin your first practice.'

3
Meanwhile, On Earth

Once the eating had begun, Lee Franks could be forgiven for forgetting all about his friend Spiky. Surrounded by other friends, and by all kinds of savouries to eat, he gave himself up to enjoying himself. Not more than twenty minutes later the plates were all empty and his dad was setting up the next stage of the party, which was the watching of comic films from a video tape. The audience had just been suitably seated when the telephone rang. Mrs Franks answered the call.

'That was Spiky's mum,' she said when she came back. 'She's just come home from work, and Spiky wasn't there. She wanted to check that he was here, because some other kids have gone missing too.'

'Oh,' said Mr Franks. He was not all that interested, because he was a Laurel and Hardy fan, and wanted the show to begin.

'Seems as though it's children from the choir that are missing,' went on Mrs Franks. 'Mrs Jackson says all the parents are creating about it.'

'Pull the other leg,' said Mr Franks. 'Let's get going. Better draw the curtains.'

So Mrs Franks obeyed her husband, and

dismissed all thought of the choir from her head. The programme was well under way, and the audience was becoming restive, to the annoyance of Mr Franks, when the doorbell rang.

'Maybe that's Spiky,' suggested Mr Franks – but it wasn't. Mr Caracco, Lee's teacher, stood at the door when Mrs Franks opened it.

'I came to enquire whether any of Mr Browser's choir happen to be here, Mrs Franks,' he asked. 'I know Lee is friendly with one or two boys in Mr Browser's class, and we are a bit worried because we can't find any of the choir.'

'Spiky's not here, Mr Caracco, and there's nobody else out of Mr Browser's class either. Mrs Jackson has been on the phone to me already.'

'It could be a very serious matter, Mrs Franks. Do you think I might have a word with the children? We want to try and discover what's happened to the choir. The police may well be calling later.'

'What's all that about?' shouted the short-tempered Mr Franks. 'We aren't hiding the school choir, if that's what you're thinking.'

'No, of course not, Mr Franks,' replied Mr Caracco as Mrs Franks grudgingly allowed him into the room. 'But the whole choir has disappeared, and we're all very concerned about it. If any of these children could give us a clue – '

Reluctantly Mr Franks switched off the programme, and the children answered Mr Caracco's questions. They had all left school promptly in order to go to the party, so they couldn't help him much. They had seen the choir assembling in the hall, and Spiky had called out to Lee that he'd be along later, and beyond that there was nothing to report.

'We're setting up an information centre at the school,' Mr Caracco informed them. 'Mr Sage will be staying there all night if necessary, so if you have any news please let us know.'

Mr Caracco rode off on his motor-bike, and Mr Franks tried his best to get the party going again. Not even the prospect of a disco could gain the full attention of the gathering now, and soon Mr Franks lost interest in the party and retired to fill in his pools coupon. Now the news that the whole choir was missing was the only subject of conversation at the party, and Lee decided that it would be more fun to join in the search than to jig around half-heartedly at a disco. So the cassette was switched off and the children dispersed, some homewards, being more interested in the rest of the evening's T.V. programmes than the remains of Lee's party, and others, like Lee, made off to Chivvy Chase School to confirm the strange story that Mr Caracco had brought.

Lee rode up the school path on his bicycle, and nobody bothered to tell him off. There were two police cars in the car park, and parents were coming and going. Lee could see Mr Sage, the Headmaster, in his room talking to two policemen. A group of parents and children, younger and older brothers and sisters of the members of the choir, was hanging around the front entrance to the school.

'Have they been found?' asked Lee, expertly circling and pulling up on his ten-gear bicycle.

'Of course they haven't!' replied a big brother irritably, scowling at Lee. 'We wouldn't be waiting here if they had.'

Lee could see that his own appearance was not at all popular when all these people wanted to see was the return of their own children.

'Can I help?' he asked, his better nature coming to the fore.

'Thanks, lad,' said Michael Fairlie's father. 'There are search parties out all over the town in cars, and the police are patrolling as well, so I don't suppose you can do much. Perhaps you could ask your dad to report to the police here with his car. They want children who know the missing ones to tour around the outlying districts of the town.'

The full seriousness of the situation then struck Lee for the first time.

'All right – I'll tell him,' he said, and rode off

at speed.

In the Headmaster's room Mr Sage was talking to the policeman who often visited Chivvy Chase School, who was there with a plain clothes detective and Mr Portland-Smythe, who as an ex-Chairman of the Parents' Association was still a person of influence about the place.

'The fact that Mr Browser's car is still in the car park implies that he has been taken by surprise, or that he has gone off with the children at short notice,' the plain clothes policeman was saying. 'Mrs Browser has reported nothing at all has been unusual about her husband of late, nor has he said anything to make her suspicious. He seems an altogether reliable, if somewhat dreamy sort of man. It's a dreadful thought, but could he possibly have gone out of his mind and forced the children away with him somewhere?'

'Without anybody seeing him?' put in Mr Sage. 'No, George Browser has always been a very calm, even-tempered man. I just can't believe he would do anything to bring harm to the children.'

'Not knowingly, I'm sure,' said the policeman irritably, and they all stared at one another, not knowing what to say next.

'He did become over serious some time back,' said Mr Portland-Smythe. 'Seemed to think his class consisted of child geniuses. But that was in the time of Mr Salt, the previous head, who was rather taken by that idea.'

'Ah yes, poor Salt,' said Mr Sage. 'He did take things most seriously at times, and I suppose it affected Mr Browser.'

'He behaved very well on our school trip to Pakistan,' went on Mr Portland-Smythe. 'Took charge of the children very ably when a certain amount of heatstroke was about.'

'Yes, indeed, it finished poor Mr Salt,' confirmed Mr Sage, showing the sympathy Headmasters have for those who have made way for themselves.

The plain clothes man wasn't getting very far.

'I still think somebody must have seen the choir leaving,' he said. 'I'd like to speak to Mr Watchett, the caretaker, again. I know he says he saw nothing, but there might be something of interest to us which he didn't regard as important enough to mention.'

Mr Watchett was duly produced.

'Now tell me, Mr Watchett, did anything at all happen after school today which doesn't normally happen? We're looking for the smallest clue, and anything might help.'

Mr Watchett frowned, and at first could recall nothing unusual. He had been working hard all the time, he told them.

'What about your cleaners?'

'The cleaners – they were busy in the rooms. Oh

yes, Doris Harrison collapsed on the path between the outside classrooms and the school. I soon brought her round. As a matter of fact, I asked her whether she'd seen the choir going home, and she said she hadn't. So she can't help you, I'm afraid. Been overworking, Doris has.'

'I'd better go and see her, nevertheless,' decided the policeman. 'Where does she live?'

The policeman left, and Mr Sage collected from his car the blankets he had brought with him from home and started to make himself a bed on the long couch which was used for sick children during school time. By now the news of the vanished choir had spread to most people connected with Chivvy Chase School, and a number of teachers, Miss Copewell the secretary and Mrs Crisp the Welfare Assistant all arrived back at school, anxious to know what was happening and to offer their assistance.

Mr Sage explained that the police had taken charge, and that not much more could be done, but his helpers insisted on staying in order to make tea and talk to anxious parents who kept on appearing from time to time.

Then the moment Mr Sage had feared arrived. A young lady journalist from the local paper knocked at his door.

'I've heard this report,' she said, 'that a whole

choir is missing, Mr Sage. Not a *whole* choir, surely?'

'I shouldn't make too much of it,' begged Mr Sage. 'They'll probably all turn up soon.'

'But a *whole* choir, and their teacher! It's unbelievable! Have they ever gone missing before?'

Mr Sage groaned, but he had to have her in and answer all her questions. He prayed that by the next evening, before the next edition of the paper came out, the choir would have returned. When she had gone, after begging Mr Sage to inform her if there were any further news, he found sitting alone in his room as hard to bear as having information squeezed out of him by the press. If the choir didn't turn up soon, he realised, the local press would not be the only ones interested. The dailies would soon seize on a story like this, followed by the T.V. cameras. He imagined himself being interviewed for a news programme.

'Don't you think it rather surprising, Mr Sage, that a school could lose a whole choir without noticing it?'

Oh dear! He stood up and went to the window, trying to imagine the police cars and the parent helpers touring the streets, fanning out ever wider – and still his phone brought no good news, only anxious enquiries. A helicopter flew low overhead, and its presence cheered him until he was beset by gloomy thoughts. If a helicopter couldn't find them, what hope would there be after that? He wished he could be out with the searchers, and paced up and down in his room with his hands behind his back and his head down. An hour later it began to grow dark, but he didn't put on the light; a bright light would only expose him more to reality, and he wanted to hide away from the truth. Mr Salt, the former Headmaster, had ended up with a nervous breakdown, and Mr Sage wondered whether he might not soon follow that example.

'Confound it, Browser – where are you?' he said aloud, and Miss Copewell came running from her office.

'Cup of tea, Mr Sage?' she asked brightly, but he waved her away as the phone rang.

'It's the Area Education Officer, Mr Sage,' announced Miss Copewell.

'Oh no! That's the last straw!' muttered Mr Sage – but of course, it wasn't by a long way.

Out in the streets the parents and their neighbours stood at their front gates talking and waiting for news from the dozens of cars which were creeping up and down the roads of the town, stopping here and there to allow children to explore the alleys which cars could not reach. The drivers shook their heads when the children returned with no news; they couldn't believe thirty or so children could hide themselves away without anyone knowing. As to what had happened to the choir, they could only shake their heads again.

When Lee returned home and told his parents that all that Mr Caracco had said was true, and that the police were searching everywhere for the choir, the good-natured side of Mr Franks took over.

'I've seen cars going up and down,' he said. 'I reckon they ought to be looking in church halls and places like that. Maybe they've gone somewhere to sing. I'll bring the Jaguar out of the garage and we'll do our bit, Lee.'

'Don't be gone too long,' called out Mrs Franks.

'We'll come back when we've found 'em,' said Mr Franks cheerfully, and roared off up the street to the envy of the neighbours. He made first for St. Margaret's Church Hall, but there he was quickly put in his place by a lady who was conducting a Yoga class.

'The police have been here already,' she told him. 'And we've had three other parents checking up as well. There are no children here, and if I were you I'd save your energy, because the police are going to all the halls in the area.'

She turned briskly back to her class, who were lying on mats with their legs in the air, waiting to be told to lie flat again.

'That's all the thanks you get for trying to help!' muttered Mr Franks, and returned to his car. 'I think they must have gone further afield,' he said to Lee. 'Let's go to the coast – you never know where they might turn up.'

This gave him the excuse to roar away at nearly eighty miles an hour along a short stretch of dual carriageway which brought him to the promenade. By now darkness was setting in. The front was deserted, and Mr Franks suddenly remembered a

T.V. programme he wanted to see.

'Reckon we can't do any more, Lee,' he decided. 'We'll make for home.'

Lee sat back as they sped homewards, wondering where his friends could be, and what Mr Caracco would do about the absence of Spiky Jackson from the football team. They turned off the main road down a street of shops and small warehouses, which boasted one supermarket standing on its own halfway down the street. As they approached it, Lee sat up straight.

'Dad! Slow down!' he called, grabbing his father's arm.

'I told you never to do that, son!' grumbled Mr Franks – but Lee was ignoring him. He was staring at the huge expanse of wall which was the side of the supermarket. Mr Franks saw a pale light shining on it, and was interested enough to slow down.

'It's them!' cried Lee. 'They're on the wall!'

Mr Franks stalled the car in his surprise. Halfway up the wall, sitting in three rows, was the Chivvy Chase School choir.

'How did they get up there?' demanded Mr Franks. 'What are they sitting on?'

He pressed the button which opened the side windows. Suddenly the choir began to sing.

'They're singing "Yellow Bird",' said Lee. 'That's one of Mr Browser's favourites.'

'Can't see him,' said Mr Franks looking on the ground beneath the wall for the conductor.

'He's not there,' decided Lee. 'They look a bit big, don't they?'

'Large as life!' agreed his father. 'Let's get going and tell the police. We've found them, Lee!'

'Go to the school,' said Lee. 'It's nearer, and there are policemen and parents waiting there.'

They were there in ninety seconds, and they found Mr Sage sitting at his desk looking at a book called *Assembly Stories,* but clearly not seeing a word.

'We've found them, Mr Sage,' cried Lee, bursting into the Headmaster's room without as much as knocking.

'Found them?' repeated Mr Sage in a daze.

'Yes – the choir. We've seen them!' announced Mr Franks, following his son into the room. Now Mr Sage sprang to his feet.

'Where? Hurry up, man – I must ring the police.'

'All right, all right, old man. Don't over excite yourself,' said Mr Franks. 'They can't run away all that quick, not from where they are.'

'Well, where are they?'

'Halfway up the wall of the supermarket in Trinity Road.'

'What?' Mr Sage, who had been wondering if he might be losing his own senses, now suspected that

SU
25.

Mr Franks had lost his.

'Up the supermarket wall, Mr Sage, honest,' put in Lee. 'They were singing "Yellow Bird".'

Lee's earnest expression and pleading tone of voice convinced Mr Sage that the matter should be looked into.

'Sit down,' he said, 'while I ring the police station.'

He soon reported that the police were sending a car to the supermarket, and requested that he go there too, with Mr Franks and Lee.

'Were they all there?' asked Mr Sage as they drove off in the Jaguar from the car park.

'Looked like it, Mr Sage,' declared Lee. 'Not Mr Browser, though. I couldn't see him anywhere.'

Mr Sage was concentrating on the choir.

'And how were they supported – halfway up the wall?'

'I couldn't see, Mr Sage. But they were there, honest they were.'

'Of course they were. I saw them too, remember,' put in Mr Franks, ever ready to take offence.

'Oh, I'm sure you did,' said Mr Sage, and they drove on in silence.

A policeman was just getting out of his car when they arrived.

'I can't see anything,' he said as Mr Franks opened the car door. 'Show me where they're supposed to be, will you?'

'Yes. Over there, up the wall,' said Mr Franks, and hurried to a position from which he could see the wall.

'Looks a very ordinary wall, to me,' said the policeman suspiciously.

'They've gone!' said Lee, and turned pale in the darkness. 'They were up there!'

He pointed, and the policeman's eyes followed the direction of the pointing finger. Then he turned to face Mr Franks.

'Now, sir,' he said, using an official tone of voice. 'I hope that you realise that to take part in a hoax, or to spread rumours is possibly criminal under circumstances like this, and is certainly very heartless towards the parents worried about their missing children.'

'Indeed,' added Mr Sage, whose fresh hope had suddenly withered away, 'I think it's unforgivable, Mr Franks.'

'Hey, wait a moment – we saw them, didn't we, Lee? We're not playing any hoax, Mr Sage. They were here, singing!'

'Well, I suppose we'd better take a look around, just to see if they've left any trace of themselves,' said the policeman grudgingly. They searched the area around the supermarket and found no sign of the missing choir. A second police car arrived with the manager of the supermarket in it, and he opened up and searched the building, also to no effect. They all came back to the cars.

'The best thing that can be said,' observed the policeman, 'is that Mr Franks and his son have been so concerned about the choir that they imagined the whole thing, with the best intentions, I hope. But we might as well go home now and forget this incident altogether!'

'Just a moment! Hang on, Officer! I've something to tell you!'

The voice was that of an old man who had come out of a flat over a small shop on the other side of the road. He came puffing up to them, then pointed to the supermarket wall.

'I saw some kids up there,' he said. 'Heard them singing, first of all. Opened the window – and there they were. Perched like birds on the side of the wall. Well, not really like birds – it was very odd, the way they were sitting there. I went to call my wife, and when we came back – they were gone!'

The policeman stared, but Lee Franks spoke up.

'What song were they singing?' he asked the old man.

'Sorry – I don't know the name of the song – but it was about a yellow bird,' said the old man.

'I told you, Mr Sage!' said the excited Lee. 'I saw them, and that was the song they were singing!'

Mr Sage was open mouthed.

'It's all very well,' said a policeman, who had been making a note in a book, 'but if you saw them, where are they now?'

Lee Franks stared at the wall, and nobody could give an answer. The supermarket wall looked down upon them, a mysterious, huge blank.

4
Choir Practice in Space

Spiky Jackson awoke to the sound of a quiet voice coming from a grill in the ceiling above his head.

'Resting time is over,' announced the voice. 'You will find food on the shelf behind your head. Eat this, and prepare to enter the cleansing department of your room. Stand in front of the button in the wall at the foot of your bed, and see that your feet are in the middle of the square marked below. Press the button, and the square will descend and you will be processed for cleanliness. You should be ready to go to the assembly hall within five minutes.'

Spiky was pleased with the idea of having breakfast in bed, and his mouth watered at the thought of real food. He turned to see what might be on offer. In a hollowed out place on the shelf were two pills, which had clearly been sent down a small chute in the wall. One pill was red and one was yellow, and Spiky had swallowed them in a couple of seconds. Although soon afterwards his hunger disappeared, it was a disappointing kind of breakfast.

He then pressed the button in the wall opposite, and sure enough the square descended, and he

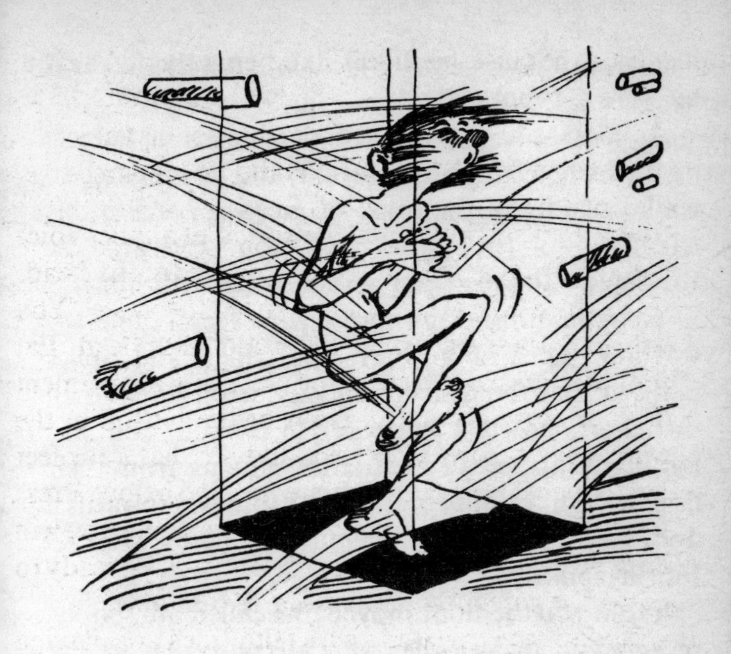

found himself in a cubicle which was a kind of shower bath. Buttons flashed and begged to be pressed, and in no time he had been washed and dried in a manner something similar to that used by an automatic car wash. Within three minutes, Spiky, dry as a bone and clean as a whistle, was standing on the square and being transported upwards again. The process was clean and quick, and no doubt washed Spiky much more efficiently than he often did himself – but he preferred his own methods, because he didn't like being treated as if he were a robot.

As soon as he was dressed, the door of his cubicle opened when he stood before it, and he prepared to walk outside, in the hope of meeting some of his friends. As he tried to step forward he stumbled – for the floor was moving with him!

'Remain still – don't move your feet!' came the warning voice of a Brain Sharpener, and Spiky realised that the instruction was being given to all the choir, not just himself. He obeyed, and was fascinated to see all his friends moving from their doorways like puppets and being directed towards a door at the far end of the corridor. Only Michael Fairlie spoke.

'I told you the floor moved,' he called out, but he received no answer; they were all trying to work out how the moving floor would bring them to the door without causing a jam of bodies.

It was easy. The floor behaved like Clapham Junction does for trains, or like a rubic cube being manipulated by a master. Gradually the children were slotted in one behind the other, until they were in a neat line as they passed through the doorway. Mr Browser was last, because the Brain Sharpeners had experienced some difficulty in providing him with shaving materials. The Brain Sharpeners, being such an advanced race, no longer grew hair on their faces, and so had to search around a little for a razor.

When they were all gathered in the Assembly Hall, the Commander appeared and announced that the Prime Brain Sharpener would shortly be appearing on the screen to inform them of what was required of them. A bell rang, and the Brain Sharpeners present turned dutifully toward the screen, on which the image of the Prime Brain Sharpener soon appeared.

'I trust that you have all slept well,' he began, in the friendly tones of an officer who is going to ask his men to carry out a specially dangerous attack. 'You will be well looked after, so that you are fresh for each session and able to perform to the best of your ability. Has anyone any complaint to make?'

Nobody had, but Anna couldn't resist the chance to say something.

'What is it you expect us to do?'

'That I am about to tell you,' said the Prime Brain Sharpener. 'You already know, I think, that you are to sing some songs for us. We wish to send a warning to Earth. We require the leaders of all countries to stop the making of those weapons which are threatening the human race and also the safety of other planets as well. The warlike spirit could easily spread from Earth to Space. New weapons are bound to be invented, and eventually they could upset the balance of things, even affecting the behaviour of your sun, thus causing a kind of domino effect in the universe. No doubt you have watched dominoes falling on television programmes. Apart from that, we wouldn't like to see your world destroyed, because you could be useful later on in helping to create a universe in which all creatures could live in peace.'

'Why not tell them that yourselves?' asked Anna. 'They won't take any notice of us.'

'That is precisely what they will do,' the Prime Brain Sharpener contradicted her. 'If we broke into human affairs directly ourselves, they would no doubt send out their rockets and bombs and try and destroy this Space Station of ours. But when they hear your voices they will listen and they will know that using force will not help. They will know that just as we have taken you from the Earth, so we shall take others if they do not see sense. Our most creative Brain Sharpeners are working on a song for you to sing to the whole people – a song which will make your rulers realise that in order to have you back on Earth they will have to come to an agreement. You will be able to sing some of your own songs too, in order to attract people's attention.'

The choir looked bewildered, and when the Prime Brain Sharpener paused, hands shot up.

'Put your hands down!' ordered the Commander, but the Prime Brain Sharpener indicated that he was ready to listen.

'Let them speak, one at a time,' he commanded. 'These children must understand what they are doing and why they are doing it.'

'Where are we going to do our singing?' asked Anna hopefully. 'They won't be able to hear us from here.'

'Of course not,' explained the Prime Brain Sharpener. 'Your images will be projected down to Earth in various places, so that very quickly many people will be able to hear you.'

Anna pouted, disappointed that she wasn't going back to Earth in person.

'What's the good,' asked Martin, 'of us only singing in English, when rockets and warheads and nuclear bombs are in other countries as well? It's no good if you only make an agreement with the English.'

'Precisely,' agreed the Prime Brain Sharpener. 'That's why you are going to have to learn our song in all kinds of languages – Russian, French, German, Chinese, Japanese – '

'But we can't speak any of those languages,' protested Spiky.

'All you have to do,' said the Prime Brain Sharpener patiently, 'is to make the sounds. Our

Creative Brain Sharpener Department will translate the song into all the different languages, and you will simply learn the words of the song. Your teacher will be instructing you, and there will be no difficulty.'

'When are we going back to Earth?' called out Spiky, voicing the question which was in all minds.

'You will return,' replied the Prime Brain Sharpener, 'when an agreement has been made and we are sure that the making of weapons of destruction will cease. If an agreement is not reached, we shall have to take further action. Now, I have given Earth enough of my time. You will go to the recording room to begin practising.'

'One more question, please!' called out Mr Browser.

'Yes?'

'The parents of the children will be very worried. You will be causing much suffering if you don't quickly allow them to know that their children are alive.'

'Oh well,' muttered the Prime Brain Sharpener to the Commander irritably, 'let them sing one of their own songs, and let their first appearance be in their own area.'

The Commander bowed low, and the Prime Brain Sharpener disappeared from the screen.

'We must now go to the recording studio in order

that you can practice,' declared the Commander, relieved to be in charge again. 'Mr Browser will select your first song, and as soon as he is satisfied with it we shall record it and relay the recording down to Earth. Then you will begin work on other songs, including the one which the Prime Brain Sharpener mentioned. Please stand on your squares.'

Once again the moving floor started juggling with its human load, and the choir was transferred to a smaller room which had evidently been set up to receive them. In it were thirty transparent containers, placed in three rows so that each row could be clearly seen. Mr Browser was led to a small raised platform in front of them – but he was not to be enclosed in one of the glass-like cases.

'Sit down,' ordered the Commander when all the members of the choir were in position. This order took them by surprise, for there appeared to be nothing to sit on, but evidently some switch had been operated, and now there was a transparent seat in each little compartment. The choir sat down, and Mr Browser was told that he could begin.

'Which song would you like to sing?' asked Mr Browser, a move which surprised the Commander.

'"Yellow Bird",' suggested Anna. 'We know it off by heart. Let's get the recording done as soon as possible. My mum will be mad that I haven't come home.'

The song ' Yellow Bird ' was agreed upon.

'You'll have to sing up,' Mr Browser warned them, 'because you're inside those cases.'

'They can sing normally,' the Commander informed him. 'Sound passes unhindered through the material. Its purpose is to record their physical images in depth.'

' Yellow Bird' was given a practice run through, and then Mr Browser was ready to record.

'You will feel slight vibrations around you,' explained the Commander, but it won't be unpleasant. I have made a number of recordings myself, so I know.'

The choir sang ' Yellow Bird ' as they had never sung it before, and Mr Browser and the Commander were pleased.

'You can relax before starting on the next song,' said the Commander. 'In a few minutes we shall be able to check over this recording. You may talk if you wish.'

'That was a funny way of recording us,' observed Spiky. 'I felt as though I had an electric shock all around me.'

'It was like sherbet fizzing all round me,' was Anna's description. 'Why did they need to do that in order to record us?'

The answer soon became clear.

'The recording is now ready,' said the Commander a few minutes later, after talking with one of the technical Brain Sharpeners. 'If you will look at the wall in front of you, and Mr Browser will stand to one side, we can show you the result.'

The light in the room became slightly brighter, and flickerings appeared on the wall, rather like the warming up pictures on a T.V. screen. Gradually the pictures took form, and behold! There was the choir sitting facing itself!

'We're in 3D!' said Spiky, and a gasp of surprise spread through the choir. Then they became silent as their large as life counterparts began singing ' Yellow Bird '.

As soon as the song was finished there was a hum of conversation.

'We're large as life!' said Martin.

'Our mums are going to think we're really back again,' said Anna. 'Only we shan't be!' She began to sniffle. 'It's cruelty!' she complained.

The Commander seemed pleased with the effect the recording had made on the choir.

'We can, of course, enlarge the figures for showing at a distance,' he told them, and waved to the technicians to demonstrate this. Then, on the wall, appeared a choir of giants, each one at least five times the natural size. When they opened their mouths to sing, the volume was tremendous.

'Enough,' said the Commander, observing that some of the choir were frightened by themselves. 'You will only be that size when we are showing you from a long distance. Most of the time you will be no larger than normal.'

'I'm glad of that,' said Spiky. 'I don't like myself, giant size.'

'Now,' went on the Commander, 'I will leave you to complete your practice. The recording will be sent down to Earth as soon as possible. It will only be shown briefly, because we want to make our biggest impact with the full recording, including our new song. Mr Browser, you may continue!'

Mr Browser, who had been amazed and disturbed by the size of the choir he had seen on the screen, was happy to have the children back at their usual size, and went on to practise a selection of the most popular songs.

The Brain Sharpeners were so pleased with the performance of the choir that they allowed the children to spend some time in the Relaxation Centre of the Outer Space Station. Evidently little Brain Sharpeners were amused by much the same things as little humans, for there were slides and areas with a trampoline effect, where you could swim in space. There were even very pleasant pills to suck, which gave a number of different tastes, including strawberry ice cream, chocolate and

orange juice.

Some of the choir were lulled into contentment.

'This is better than a holiday in Spain,' said Martin, who often liked to bring his stay in Benidorm into the conversation.

'You always come home after a holiday in Spain,' said Anna.

'Well, we ought to be able to go home soon. They seem to be pleased with us,' said her friend Thelma.

'But we have to learn all those languages first,' Spiky reminded them. 'And even then, who knows if the people on Earth are going to do what the Brain Sharpeners want? They can be very obstinate.'

Nobody did know, and somehow the taste of the pills became less delightful, and the slides and the swimming in space lost their appeal.

'I want to go home,' whimpered Anna – and so did the rest, though they didn't say so aloud.

5
The Choir Becomes Famous

'You have to believe us now,' said Mr Franks to the policeman. 'I wouldn't make up a story like that – the kids in the choir are Lee's friends.'

'I appreciate that,' said the policeman. 'We shall be making more enquiries in the area, but we would be obliged if you and your son kept quiet about what you say you saw. We don't want to build up false hopes in people's minds.'

'You still aren't sure of us,' grumbled Mr Franks.

'It's not that, sir – but where have those children gone? You must admit that you don't know.'

Lee's father had to agree, and he promised to keep quiet about the appearance of the choir until further notice. When he had taken Lee home in his car he had to go out for a drink with some of his friends to help him recover from the shock and to resist the temptation to talk about the choir.

The police began knocking up householders in the area in the hope of discovering more evidence. The result was confusing. Several people had heard the choir singing, but no one had seen the singers. They assumed that the singing must have come from someone else's radio.

Mr Sage went back to Chivvy Chase School, and parents who had been alerted by his absence were disappointed to hear that there was no further news, for Mr Sage had also been advised to say nothing. He slept uneasily in the school medical room, and in the morning he had to begin answering questions all over again. By now the local radio station was on to the story – indeed, the police had requested them to make a broadcast asking for help from anyone who might have any idea of the whereabouts of the choir. This, in turn, brought the attention of the national newspapers to the disappearance, and poor Mr Sage was being interviewed in his room most of the afternoon by journalists and education officials, none of whom could understand how the Headmaster could possibly have lost a whole choir.

The Headmaster of Lower Lane School, a rival school at the other end of the town, and the winners of the Choir Festival for the past two years, rang up to ask Mr Sage if he were trying to gain publicity for his new choir, and in spite of all Mr Sage's protests, couldn't believe any more than the journalists that it was possible to lose a whole choir.

Lee Franks was hard put to it not to tell his friends about the appearance of the choir on the supermarket wall, but his task was made easier because the more time passed the less he could believe in his own story himself.

Again the next night Mr Sage slept in the school, though this time he had no helpers staying late to make him tea. On the following day the worst, for Mr Sage, happened. The crew of a T.V. programme called 'Countrywide' turned up at the school and requested to be allowed to film the school, especially the hall from which the choir had disappeared, and then to hold interviews with Mr Sage, the caretaker and one or two parents of missing children. Mr Sage would dearly have liked to say no, but he was overruled by officials above him, who preferred to let Mr Sage talk rather than have to do so themselves.

Poor Mrs Browser had her house ransacked by the police, who were searching for any signs of her husband being odd. They read through his personal diaries, and only came across one suspicious entry from some time back: 'Thank goodness the Brain Sharpeners have gone!'

Mrs Browser couldn't help them at all as to what this might mean.

'I expect he's referring to the inspectors,' she said in desperation at last. The police finally went away, disappointed that they could pin nothing on Mr Browser.

That evening Mr Sage went home for the first time and watched himself on T.V. He thought he had done rather well to fend off all the awkward questions put to him, though his wife upset him afterwards.

'You did look pale,' she said. 'And you didn't know anything!'

'Well, that's the truth!' declared Mr Sage. 'I don't know anything. Who does?'

The headlines in the newspapers the next day did nothing to improve his spirits. They read: 'SCHOOL LOSES CHOIR.' 'HEADMASTER

ADMITS CHOIR VANISHED.' 'CHOIR LOST WITHOUT TRACE.' 'NO CLUES IN MISSING CHOIR CASE.'

Poor Mr Sage! He would have liked to close down the school, but he knew that to do so would only bring more headlines. How he wished that the choir would return – but if it didn't, then he hoped that all the fuss would gradually die down. His wishes were not to be granted. At three o'clock that afternoon the phone rang and Miss Copewell reported that the police wanted to speak to him. Mr Sage hurried to his room.

'Mr Sage? We've news of your choir.'

'Yes?' Mr Sage was bursting with hope.

'Yes, they've been seen on the white cliffs of Dover, singing a selection of songs. Some people in a fishing boat were the first to see them, and it's been confirmed by a speedboat which was sent out immediately.'

'Wonderful,' said Mr Sage. 'You said they were on top of the cliffs?'

'Not exactly. The face of the cliffs was mentioned. They stood out against the chalk. Perhaps you could come round here – we're awaiting further details. If they're found, we'll take you straight down to Dover. We have to be careful, though, because of the rumour we had the other night.'

'I'll be round at once,' promised Mr Sage, and rushed out of his room and the school without as much as telling Miss Copewell where he was going.

At the police station he made himself known to the officer on duty, who quickly transferred him to a little room behind the scenes. The detective in charge of the case rose to meet him.

'Good news, I hear,' Mr Sage greeted him.

'I'm afraid it's not so good,' was the reply. 'Please sit down, Mr Sage. I have to tell you that as we were making an attempt to approach the cliff, the choir disappeared. I received a phone call to that effect shortly after we had rung you.'

Mr Sage put his hands to his head.

'Another hoax, then! But why?'

'We don't know if it was a hoax – there appears to be no reason for the people concerned to make up their story. What's more, we have already had further news of another appearance of the choir.'

'Another one?'

'Yes. This time the children were sighted on an unused bandstand in the seaside town of Rocksea. We understand that a number of people watched and listened to them, thinking that a school choir had taken over the bandstand for a practice. The witnesses could say exactly which songs were sung. Among them were "The Skye Boat Song", "Strawberry Fair" and "Yellow Bird".'

'That could be my choir,' admitted Mr Sage. 'But lots of choirs sing those songs.'

'Agreed,' said the detective. 'But choirs don't usually vanish at the end of their performances, which is becoming a habit with yours. That's what happened at Rocksea, according to the witnesses. One minute the choir was there, the next it was gone. It was then that one of the witnesses thought about the Chivvy Chase Choir and rang the police.'

At this point the phone rang, and the detective carried on a conversation in which his part was mostly a listening one. He was frowning when he put down the receiver.

'The choir has been heard singing outside Edinburgh Castle,' he said. 'Hundreds of people saw the children this time. They were singing the same songs, in the same order.'

'Didn't anyone go to them?' asked the bewildered Headmaster.

'They were in a position difficult to reach, and when an attempt was made to approach them, the whole choir disappeared.'

The detective and Mr Sage stared at one another.

'It's uncanny,' said Mr Sage.

'Indeed it is,' agreed the detective. 'Your choir is certainly becoming famous.'

Mr Sage returned to school and said nothing about all he had heard. But in the morning, when he

opened his newspaper, he realised that nothing could be kept secret any longer. 'SCHOOL CHOIR REAPPEARS,' screamed the headlines. 'CHOIR'S CAT AND MOUSE GAME.' 'HIDE AND SEEK CHOIR.' 'COUNTRYWIDE SIGHTINGS OF MISSING CHOIR.'

The choir, it was reported, had been seen and heard in the following places: Dover, Edinburgh, Rocksea, Plymouth, Stonehenge, Manchester, Norwich (in the castle grounds), Scarborough (on top of the Grand Hotel), Bournemouth (in the bandstand in the gardens near the Pavilion), Liverpool (on the end of the football ground known as 'The Kop'), and on top of colleges in Oxford and Cambridge. In each case the choir disappeared before anyone could come near. The children were reported as real – as large as life, or even larger, as one witness described them.

Some of the papers, Mr Sage discovered, had serious articles about the choir, in which they tried to find explanations of the strange phenomenon. The explanations offered were based mostly on the idea that somebody was playing a technical hoax on the whole country – that perhaps some big firm had perfected a new technique and was using the choir as a huge free advertisement before revealing what their product was.

At Chivvy Chase School a meeting of excited parents was held, and some of them went so far as to accuse Mr Sage of being hand in glove with the supposed firm, which he fiercely denied.

'Why is it the choir hasn't appeared here?' demanded one father angrily, and then Lee Franks's father could remain silent no longer.

'The choir has been seen here,' he announced. 'The first appearance was here, but nobody would believe Lee and me – we saw them, Mr Sage knows that, but we were told not to speak.'

The hall buzzed with excitement, outrage and hostility.

'Our children appeared, and you didn't tell us?' shouted one mum at Mr Sage. The meeting was calmed by none other than the Chief Education

Officer, who had come from as far off as County Headquarters in order to be present.

'I call on Mr Sage to make a statement,' he said.

'Your children were seen,' confirmed Mr Sage, 'but by the time the police arrived on the scene they had disappeared, and at that stage we could not be sure that the sighting was genuine. We did not wish to raise false hopes. I also wish to deny absolutely that there is any known connection with any advertising campaign. How could you possibly believe that I would do a thing like that, ladies and gentlemen? I beg you to believe that I am as upset and mystified about what is going on as you are yourselves. We must be patient and take comfort from the fact that the choir must be somewhere, since they have been heard singing in various places.'

The meeting broke up in confusion, and there was still some grumbling about the school from those parents who had grown used to grumbling over the years.

At Scotland Yard plans were devised so that fast cars were made available to be rushed to the next spot where the choir might appear, and also helicopters were standing by so that men could be lowered amongst the children should the choir be spotted high up on a building.

In Parliament the Member for the Chivvy Chase area was pleased to stand up and ask an awkward question of the Home Secretary, demanding to know what was being done and how much longer the poor parents would have to suffer.

'I can assure the Honourable Member,' said the Home Secretary, 'that everything possible is being done to return the children to their parents and to bring to justice those responsible for this heartless affair.'

'What exactly is being done?' roared a few of his enemies.

'It is a curious fact,' he replied, 'that there has so

far been no appearance of the choir in London. Should that happen, Scotland Yard is ready to act immediately, and I am confident that the mystery will be quickly solved.'

'You don't know what's going on!' shouted one member rather rudely, and secretly most of the M.P.s agreed with him, but there was little that anyone could do, so they went on to discuss other important matters, such as how many pigs should be allowed in a field of a certain size, and how many children a beach donkey should be allowed to carry in one day.

'This, of course,' one M.P. was droning away, 'must depend on the size and weight of the children – '

At this point an excited official handed a message to Mr Speaker, who coughed and begged to make an announcement.

'I have to inform you,' he said, 'that the choir of Chivvy Chase School is performing at the moment on the roof of this House – between the entrance for members and the entrance to the Public Galleries. I shall accordingly adjourn the House – '

But by the time he had finished saying that, all the few M.P.s left were on their feet and hurrying for the exits. Outside, a crowd was gathering, and all traffic on the roads around had to be diverted, or London would have come to a standstill. In the distance the sirens of police cars wailed. Important policemen were hurrying from Scotland Yard not far away.

The Chivvy Chase School choir was singing 'The Skye Boat Song', and when they finished it the crowd applauded. The police were annoyed with the crowd, which was getting in the way of their cars. A helicopter, in radio contact with the Police Commissioner, appeared in the distance. The choir sang 'Under the Linden Tree', and by the time that was finished the helicopter was overhead, ready to send down two daring members of the S.A.S., armed to the teeth, who were going to rescue the choir from – what?

Then a boy in the front row of the choir stood up – a boy with a spike of hair standing up straight. Spiky Jackson began to speak, reading from a piece of what looked like paper.

'We are now going to sing a new song,' he announced. 'Please listen to it carefully, for it contains a message to you from the Brain Sharpeners. When it is finished, we shall disappear, but one of us will be coming back to Earth to make our Government an offer from the Brain Sharpeners. If that offer is not accepted, action will be taken to make sure that this country has no power to disturb the world or space around it. The same will apply to all other countries, which will have to learn from this example, and will be treated in the same way. The Brain Sharpeners wish to live in peace, as their song will tell you. Please listen to the Chivvy Chase School choir now.'

Spiky had been speaking with precision and clarity, as though his voice were not his own. The S.A.S. men prepared to descend, but the Police Commissioner had received instructions from the Government and flashed them a message that they should delay.

'Perhaps we had better listen to the song,' suggested the Home Secretary, who was feeling most disturbed and puzzled as he wondered what these Brain Sharpeners might be able to do. Spiky sat down and the choir began to sing:

'Far from the land where we belong
To people on the Earth we sing this song –
From distant realms of Outer Space
We bring this warning to the Human Race.
The Brain Sharpeners warn you
Their message rings clear –
Obey their instructions
Or danger is near –
So beware, please beware!

Your rockets and your missiles fly
Beyond the regions which you call the sky –
Soon you could threaten us – or worse,
Upset the balance of the Universe!
The Brain Sharpeners warn you
Their message rings clear –
Their world could be threatened,
They must interfere!
So beware, please beware!

A messenger they'll send you
To tell your leaders what to do
If you desire your world to be
A planet which can still be free.
The Brain Sharpeners warn you
Their message rings clear –
Invade Space with missiles
Your world's end draws near!
So beware, please beware!'

The song was sung without feeling, unlike the others, as though the choir was reluctant to sing it. The rhythm was slow, as if inviting the listeners to think about their own fate rather than concentrate on the song. The crowd, at the end of it, seemed hypnotised into silence. And as suddenly as the choir had appeared, it was gone.

When the helicopter descended, and men

swarmed over the building, examining it for any traces of the choir, it was all too late; not a clue was to be found. An angry man forced his way to the front of the crowd by the railings of Parliament, and shouted to the pressmen and a group of M.P.s who were gathered inside the railings.

'That was my son, Simon Jackson, in the choir. Why don't you do something about it? Somebody's playing a cruel trick, and the Government must make him pay! If the Government don't bring the whole choir back, I say the Government must resign!'

Some of the crowd growled their agreement, though most were still trying to explain to themselves what had happened. The M.P.s stood silently, until one asked Mr Jackson to hand in his name and address, and promised that a Question would be asked in the House.

'A question! It's not a question I want, it's an answer,' grumbled Spiky's father.

The M.P. shook his head at Mr Jackson's unreasonableness, and he was taken over by the pressmen, who were now recovering themselves and trying to work out the meaning of the choir's last song. By the time the evening papers came out, they had decided that the magical appearance and disappearance of the choir couldn't simply be a hoax, and in spite of the worries of Government

officials, they brought the Brain Sharpeners out into the open for the first time with headlines such as these:

'BRAIN SHARPENERS THREATEN EARTH!'

'CHOIR SINGS MESSAGE FROM SPACE.'

And in the morning the daily papers continued in a similar way:

'CHOIR SPEAKS FOR SPACEMEN.'

'BRAIN SHARPENERS DEMAND PEACE.'

'NO MORE MISSILES, WARN BRAIN SHARPENERS.'

'SPACE HOSTAGES SING WORLD WARNING.'

Even *The Times* gave a big headline to the affair!

'GOVERNMENT THREATENED BY BRAIN SHARPENERS.'

By the end of the next day the whole of the British public was made aware that somewhere, out in space, there could well be a civilisation superior to their own.

And all the parents of the choir signed a petition demanding that the Government do something about their missing children. Mr Sage, who now felt a little less guilty about what had happened, gladly signed it too.

6
A Message from Space

'To make sure that we are believed,' said the Prime Brain Sharpener, 'it will be necessary for one of us to go to Earth and talk to their leaders. If the choirmaster goes too, there will be evidence that the children are still alive. Their leaders must be made to agree to our terms – that no more objects of any kind are to be sent beyond the oxygen belt that surrounds the Earth. We know that so far most of these objects are harmless, but we cannot risk leaving an agreement for much longer, for who knows what the Earthling researchers will produce next? If we cannot force an agreement now, we must make them understand that we shall have to invade in order to sharpen their brains to a state required by us – that is to say, dull their technical ability and increase their sense of responsibility to others.'

The conference of Brain Sharpeners applauded, but a young Brain Sharpener, hoping one day to be given a position of power, put a question.

'The country concerned is not the most powerful in this respect,' he said. 'Can we be sure that other, bigger countries will take notice of our warning?'

The Prime Brain Sharpener nodded approval.

'A good question,' he said. 'We aim to broadcast the same message to all countries on Earth, but first the choir must learn to sing our song in all the other languages, for one great drawback of civilisation on Earth is that there are so many different ones. What progress is being made in this?' he asked the Commander.

'Slow progress,' answered the Commander honestly. 'At the rate we are progressing at the moment, all languages will not have been mastered within the next ten Earth years. It takes so long for them to get the sounds right – and their choir master cannot help them, except in German and French. I am afraid we have overestimated the power of their brains.'

The Prime Brain Sharpener frowned.

'It may well be that we shall have to use other methods to warn other nations,' he admitted. 'Perhaps by capturing choirs in each country, or, to save time, going straight for their leaders.'

'We agree!' said one or two of the younger Brain Sharpeners, but the Prime Brain Sharpener was not pleased.

'We have to do all this if possible without frightening the Earthlings,' he said. 'We must at first try to reach a peaceful settlement with them. Please check up on the choir, and if necessary give them extra periods of brain sharpening. Evidently young Earthlings are slower to learn than we hoped, when they are removed from their own surroundings.'

The conference broke up, and the Brain Sharpener in charge of the choir went at once to see how work was progressing. What he saw when he reached the room where the choir was supposed to be practising would not have been thought possible by any Brain Sharpener. Spiky Jackson was rolling on the ground enjoying a friendly fight with Michael Fairlie. Anna Cardwell was making faces at Selwyn Jordan, the only member of the choir who was sitting still. Others were playing hopscotch on the Brain Sharpeners' floor, and Martin was rolling some marbles which had been in his pocket when he was kidnapped. Two technical Brain Sharpeners came out of their cells and looked on in amazement. Disorder was unknown to the Brain Sharpeners, and now the room resembled Classroom 8 at Chivvy Chase School on a wet playtime when Mr Browser was elsewhere.

The Brain Sharpener in charge at once looked for Mr Browser – but he was not to be seen.

'Silence!' demanded the Brain Sharpener in a stern voice which any teacher would have envied. 'Sit down. Why are you not practising?'

'Mr Browser has not arrived yet,' explained

Anna. 'We're supposed to start singing your song in Japanese this time, but without Mr Browser we haven't any words.'

To tell the truth, the choir was utterly fed up with having to sing the same tune over and over again, even if the words were different. Also, singing words which you can't understand can soon become boring, especially when back in England you are accustomed to everything you have to learn being made interesting.

The Brain Sharpener made no answer, but went to the wall and pressed buttons which caused a young Brain Sharpener to go and investigate why Mr Browser was not present. He soon discovered that Mr Browser was lying on his bed in his cubicle groaning.

'What is the matter? Why are you not with the singers?' asked the young Brain Sharpener.

'I am in pain,' said Mr Browser irritably. 'I am ill.'

'Ill? What is that?'

'Not well,' said Mr Browser, his hand on his stomach. 'Something is wrong.'

The young Brain Sharpener was confused.

'I will report,' he said, and did so. The news led to a quick discussion amongst the Super Top Brain Sharpeners, one of whom came to see Mr Browser in person.

'Illness,' he explained, 'is something about which

we have no experience. Ages ago, when our civilisation was young, things did go wrong with us at times, but we live in such a way now that we develop perfectly, and so know no pain.'

'You're lucky,' said Mr Browser.

'No,' said the Brain Sharpener, 'it is not luck. Our minds have outlawed illness. One of your writers on Earth, Samuel Butler, wrote that illness should be looked upon as a crime. We think he is right.'

'Thanks very much,' said Mr Browser, and groaned. 'That doesn't help me. I think I may have appendicitis – it runs in the family. I need a doctor.'

‘We have no doctors,’ said the Brain Sharpener.

‘What! And you’re supposed to be so clever!’ grumbled Mr Browser desperately.

‘We do not need them,’ the Brain Sharpener reminded him.

‘Then you will have to send me back where I can see one,’ declared Mr Browser. ‘Isn’t there anything you can do?’

The Brain Sharpener went away and came back with some apparatus and a couple of technical Brain Sharpeners.

‘We are going to have a look through you,’ he said.

‘Ah – a kind of X-Ray,’ said Mr Browser hopefully. ‘That’s a good idea.’

They placed the machine over him and the X-Ray was quickly completed.

‘There’s a funny little thing curled up on your right side, and it looks very swollen,’ announced the Brain Sharpener.

‘That’s it,’ said Mr Browser. ‘That’s my appendix. You’ll have to take it out.’

The Brain Sharpeners held a conference, involving the Super Top Brain Sharpeners.

‘We will not risk removing this thing, because we do not know how the human body will react when not on Earth,’ the Brain Sharpener informed Mr Browser after a while. ‘As we wish to send a messenger to Earth, you can go with him and introduce him to your leaders.'

'But I can hardly walk now, and if I don't have the operation quickly I could be in worse trouble,' explained Mr Browser. 'You'd better find someone else to introduce your messenger.'

A further discussion took place.

'We have decided we will send one of your singers with you,' announced the Brain Sharpener. 'The boy who announced your songs will do.'

'Simon Jackson,' said Mr Browser. 'Spiky. Yes, he will do. But please hurry up. The pain is getting worse, and it must take us a while to travel back to Earth.'

The Brain Sharpener smiled. Brain Sharpeners don't do this often, and this was a smile of superiority – but at least it was a smile.

'Five minutes of your time, now that we know how to adjust your bodies,' he said.

Spiky Jackson was delighted to hear that he was bound for home, but sorry to be leaving his friends behind and worried as to whether he would have to come back again. Mr Browser was conveyed to a small pepperpot space vehicle, and given a message to deliver to Mr Sage.

'But I can hardly walk,' protested Mr Browser.

'That's why the boy is with you,' he was told. 'He

will deliver the message and tell your Headmaster where you are. Our messenger will at once depart and hover in the region of the Houses of Parliament, where he will address your leaders when they have arrived. After dark the boy will then rejoin our space vehicle and be brought back with another teacher to take your place. If the agreement with us has been signed by your leaders, then the whole choir may be able to return.'

'So I do have to go back!' complained Spiky.

'As part of the agreement,' said the Brain Sharpener. 'You must trust us, and we will trust you.'

'My dad will be mad,' objected Spiky, trying to think of a way to change the Brain Sharpeners' minds.

'He won't know you're there,' declared the Brain Sharpener. 'Your Headmaster will have instructions to hide you away until it is time to return. Your only task is to make sure that Mr Browser is found quickly.'

'I've a good mind to run away,' muttered Spiky.

'If you do, the fate of the whole choir could be at risk. But don't worry – we shall have enough control of your brain to make you do exactly as we want.'

So Spiky and Mr Browser, in the company of an important Super Top Brain Sharpener, were

transported back to Earth, and just before the close of school one afternoon Spiky found himself standing on the school field, with Mr Browser lying on the ground next to him.

'Oh dear,' groaned Mr Browser, 'my stomach hurts more now that I'm back on Earth. Quick, hurry with this message to Mr Sage, and tell him to call for an ambulance.'

Spiky took the manuscript and ran across the empty field, his legs heavy and his arm movements stiff as he breathed Earth's impure atmosphere once more. The school was in slumbrous mood, as are most schools five minutes before the end of the afternoon, and no one took any notice of Spiky as he sped past classroom windows and went in at the main entrance. Miss Copewell did look up from her typewriter as he passed the office.

'My goodness,' she said, 'for a moment I thought I saw Simon Jackson go by.'

Mrs Crisp shook her head.

'Wishful thinking,' she said, and Miss Copewell continued typing a list of names for the school play.

Mr Sage was tidying up his desk, because he hoped to be able to leave early for his first game of golf since the disappearance of the choir. Life has to go on, and Mr Sage now tended to be happier away from Chivvy Chase School, in places where he could try and forget all the fuss over the missing children for a while. Someone came running along the corridor, thereby breaking a school rule. Mr Sage put on his sternest expression. Worse still was to follow. His door was flung open without any attempt at a knock.

Spiky Jackson stood breathlessly before him.

'Simon Jackson! Where have you come from?' asked Mr Sage, hardly knowing what he was saying and expecting Spiky to disappear at any moment.

'I've come from the Brain Sharpeners,' said Spiky. 'Mr Browser's ill on the field. Please ring for an ambulance. He thinks he has appendi – appen – '

'Appendicitis!' said Mr Sage. 'And the rest of the choir?' he asked hopefully. Spiky shook his head.

'Read this,' he said, and passed the manuscript across.

Mr Sage read, and beads of perspiration dotted his brow. It was clear that there would be no golf for him that evening, and it was also clear that, if he wasn't careful, he would find himself up in space with the choir. As if in a trance, he dialled 999. Then he remembered that Spiky was still visible, and quickly ordered him across the corridor and into the stock cupboard.

'You'll have to stay there until this evening,' he told him. 'When everybody's gone, I'll bring you something to eat and drink.'

He pushed the protesting Spiky inside.

'I'm back on Earth - let me go home,' pleaded Spiky pitifully, but fear lent Mr Sage strength, and he wasn't going to risk upsetting the Brain Sharpeners. He gave Spiky a push and locked the door on him. Breathing a sigh of relief, he went back to his desk and rang the police station, requesting them to put him in touch with the Prime Minister, either at Parliament or 10 Downing Street. By now, the strangest call from Chivvy Chase School was treated with the utmost urgency, and in a flash Mr Sage's message was passed on to the right quarter. Within a few minutes the Whips, as they are called, were summoning all members of their parties to come to the Great Hall at Westminster in order to listen to an important message from a high ranking Brain Sharpener. They were sworn to the utmost secrecy. Not even a Brain Sharpener was to be given the honour of speaking in the House of Commons itself - a privilege not even granted to Presidents of the United States. But any attempt to lessen the importance of the Brain Sharpeners, they were soon to find out, was ridiculous.

Meanwhile Mr Sage suddenly recalled that Spiky had told him that Mr Browser was out on the field, and his presence had already been spotted by children in the upper classrooms. Hurrying past the office, Mr Sage called to Miss Copewell: 'Mr

Browser's on the field – hurt, I think. Better bring Mrs Crisp out!'

'Oh dear – what next!' said Miss Copewell, and she grabbed the First Aid Box and hurried after him with Mrs Crisp at her heels. They all met Mr Caracco at the foot of the stairs.

'Mr Browser's lying on the field!' he greeted them. 'Looks to be injured. Who put him there, I wonder?'

'Come with me,' said Mr Sage, ignoring the question. 'We may have to carry him in. I've called for an ambulance.'

'But where's he come from?' insisted Mr Caracco as they jogged out on the field.

'How should I know?' answered Mr Sage grumpily – and at that moment it occurred to him that he might have a use for Mr Caracco later on, so he spoke to him in more friendly terms. 'We'll have to ask him,' he added.

Mr Browser was lying on the field groaning. 'It's the appendix, I think,' he said. 'They gave me a sort of X-Ray, and it showed up on it.'

'They? Who?' asked Mr Caracco.

'Never mind that,' replied Mr Sage, remembering the order that he should preserve secrecy. 'I've sent for an ambulance. Best thing is for you to wait here until they come with a stretcher.'

'It's so nice to see you back, Mr Browser,' said

Miss Copewell. 'Where have you been? You could have sent a postcard or something – '

Mr Sage glowered at her, but he needn't have done, for at this point Mr Browser closed his eyes and was clearly in no condition to answer any more questions. Very quickly the ambulance arrived in the car park and Mr Browser was carried away on a stretcher by two surprised ambulance men who knew that Mr Browser had been with the missing choir. Mr Browser did open his eyes just before being put in the ambulance.

'Please let my wife know I'm back,' he said.

'Where's the choir, Mr Browser?' asked Mr Caracco bluntly, but he received no answer; Mr

Browser's eyes closed again, and he was driven off to the Chivvy Chase Hospital. Mr Sage, Mr Caracco, Miss Copewell and Mrs Crisp returned to school, the last three silent and mystified.

'Mr Caracco,' said Mr Sage, 'would you mind coming to my room for a moment?'

Mr Sage closed the door of his room tightly.

'Chris,' he said, using Mr Caracco's Christian name for the first time, 'you're a very promising teacher. I've been thinking of giving you promotion for some time, for the work you've done in football and music.'

Mr Caracco was pleased to hear this.

'And I can see my way to doing this very soon, if all goes well,' continued the Headmaster.

'Thank you very much, Mr Sage.'

'You deserve it, Chris. By the way, I wonder if you could help me out this evening? There's a little job you could do for me – it might mean travelling away for a few days. I can't afford to leave the school, and you're a single man, who might not mind something of an adventure – isn't that right?'

'Well,' said Mr Caracco, thinking of his girl friend, 'I don't – '

'I don't think you'll be away for long,' Mr Sage said reassuringly. 'Just a few days until things have been sorted out. I'll call in Mrs Belchance to take your class.'

'Oh!' Mr Caracco was now a little suspicious, because he knew that Mrs Belchance could only be called in if a teacher was going to be away for at least three days.

'Where am I going?' he asked.

'Oh, don't worry,' said Mr Sage sensing the trouble. 'I can call a teacher in to Chivvy Chase School now for the slightest thing. Nothing's too good at the moment for Chivvy Chase. Why, they're even going to redecorate the school soon – oh yes, I'll tell you this evening what the task is, Chris. There's a bit of secrecy about it, you see.'

Mr Carraco was still suspicious, but the thought of sudden unexpected promotion overcame his doubts.

'May I take my guitar with me?' he asked.

'Why not,' said the friendly Mr Sage.

So Mr Caracco was destined to be the first man to take a guitar with him into Space.

7
Headlines in the Papers

'Spiky Jackson came with me!' mumbled Mr Browser as the calming drug began to take effect.

'Hear that!' said the patient in the next bed when the nurse came by. 'That's the missing teacher, isn't it? And he just said somebody came back with him.'

'Who?' asked the nurse.

'Spiky Jackson,' said the patient.

'That's a boy,' said the nurse. 'One of the choir. I wonder where he is!'

She looked at Mr Browser, to see if he might add to his statement, but he was already only semi-conscious, and ready to be wheeled into the operating room.

'He didn't say a thing to the police,' said the nurse. 'Maybe this is important.'

So she told the sister in charge of the ward, and the sister rang the police and told them what Mr Browser was supposed to have said.

'Don't tell anyone else,' said the detective who answered the phone, and immediately contacted Mr Sage. They were surprised to find that he was still at school, and set out for Chivvy Chase at once.

Much was happening at this time. The Brain

Sharpener was addressing a secret meeting of Members of Parliament in the Great Hall, informing them that if they didn't stop sending up missiles and rockets and satellites into Space the Brain Sharpeners would have to take matters into their own hands and assume control of all countries in which such materials existed. Moreover, all research into deadly weapons must stop.

'Your children will be returned only when this agreement has been signed,' declared the Brain Sharpener, and passed a manuscript to the nearest M.P.

If he thought the document was going to be signed quickly he was much mistaken. There followed a long discussion in which those who favoured signing were accused of being under the influence of the Brain Sharpeners already.

'We are only a small country,' objected one M.P.

'All countries will be dealt with in the same way,' the Brain Sharpener informed him. 'You must decide quickly, for I have to return shortly. Agree, or your children will never come back – and all the people will be told exactly why they won't return.'

At the same time poor Mr Sage was feeding chocolate, fruit and lemonade to Spiky in the stock room, and wondering whether he was doing right to keep Spiky's arrival a secret, or whether he should risk the wrath of the Brain Sharpeners and declare

Spiky's presence to the police. If he did, he realised that the whole choir might be gone for ever; on the other hand, if Spiky were to be seen, no one would believe his story and he would quite possibly be set upon by angry parents for allowing the boy to disappear again.

Just before dark Mr Caracco appeared with his guitar. By this time he had decided that in spite of Mr Sage's good intentions towards him, he wanted a quick explanation of the mystery.

'Tell me what it's all about,' he demanded, 'or I'll ride my motor-bike straight home.'

'Come with me,' said Mr Sage, who was by now glad to have someone to talk to, and he took Mr Caracco from his room to the stock room.

'Simon Jackson,' he said. 'Back from Space, brought by a Brain Sharpener.'

'Hullo, Spiky,' said Mr Caracco.

'Hullo,' replied Spiky, showing no emotion.

'He has to go back,' explained Mr Sage. He brought Mr Browser back because he's ill, and we've made an agreement that Simon should return.'

'That's hard,' said Mr Caracco.

'Maybe. But if he doesn't go, there'll be less chance of ever seeing the choir again. The Brain Sharpener is coming for him as soon as it is dark and he's finished his own business.'

'What's that?' asked Mr Caracco bluntly.

'Arranging a peace agreement,' said Mr Sage. 'The point is, Caracco, that somebody has to go back with the boy and take Browser's place. It won't be for long – but we can't possibly have the choir left on its own, can we?'

'Suppose they don't come to an agreement?'

'Oh, they must, they must. You said you'd do this for me, Caracco. I can't possibly leave myself – I have parents knocking at my door all day long asking about their children, and if I disappeared there'd be uproar.'

Fortunately for Mr Sage, apart from feeling tired of teaching Class 7, and apart from the promise Mr Sage had made to him, Mr Caracco had just endured an awful quarrel with his girl friend, who wanted him to give up playing his guitar. Perhaps already a little under the influence of the Brain Sharpeners, Mr Caracco had stormed out of the room, saying: 'All right – if I can't play the guitar here, I'll play it somewhere else!'

So as he stood before Mr Sage the prospect of flying off into Space was less upsetting to him than it might have been normally.

'All right – I promised,' he said to Mr Sage.

'Then we'd better make our way as secretly as possible out on the field,' said Mr Sage. 'We can't afford to allow anyone else to have a close-up of Simon.'

'The gardener's shed would be a good place,' suggested Mr Caracco.

'Good idea. We'll wait in there. Let's go now – come along, Simon!'

Spiky was still under the influence of the Brain Sharpeners, his brain ready to accept any message of which they approved, so he went meekly between them out to the gardener's shed, which Mr Sage unlocked with one of his many keys. A quarter of an hour passed, and darkness was falling. Mr Caracco, who was half inclined to believe that poor Mr Sage was slightly unbalanced because of the disappearance of the choir, began to hope that nothing would happen and that after an hour or so they would be able to go home.

Suddenly there was a whirring noise above him, and just as suddenly Mr Sage grabbed Spiky's hand and pulled him out on the field. A warm wind blew on their faces, and then, dimly, in the middle of the field, was the Brain Sharpener stepping out of the tiny pepperpot machine.

'Goodbye,' said Mr Sage to Spiky and Mr Caracco, 'and good luck. I hope I'll be seeing you again soon.'

The Brain Sharpener glided rather than strode straight up to Mr Sage.

'No agreement has been reached,' he said, a

hostile sneer on his face. 'I have never met with such a short-sighted, childish gathering as that I have just left. I walked out in disgust.'

'I'm sorry about that,' said Mr Sage.

'Measures will be taken,' threatened the Brain Sharpener. 'Important people will disappear. Control will be taken over by us, the people will become the slaves of the Brain Sharpeners – '

'There's a police car coming down the road!' called out Spiky.

'We will go,' said the Brain Sharpener.

'Goodbye,' said Mr Sage again, and made to draw back. The Brain Sharpener stared at him, and Mr Sage's brain crackled as if with electricity running through it. Under the withering stare of the Brain Sharpener he obediently followed Mr Caracco and Spiky into the pepperpot.

It took off just as the police car drew up in the school car park. The puzzled policemen could find no sign of Mr Sage or of Spiky, nor could they find anything untoward in the whole school. Later on they discovered that the groundsman's shed was open, but Mr Watchett, when called, admitted that his colleague might possibly have forgotten to close it.

'Can it be,' asked one policeman of another, 'that this Browser has been fooling with us? If so, something must be done!'

Later that night they received a phone call from the worried Mrs Sage, whose husband had disappeared without trace. Soon a similar call came from Mr Caracco's landlady.

'He's quarrelled with his girl friend,' she said. 'I'm afraid he may have done something silly. Or it may be something to do with that school. They ought to close it down, I say.'

Policemen hurried to the hospital to interview Mr Browser, but that wasn't possible because he was still coming round after his operation.

In the morning, faced with these fresh disappearances, the Education Officer did as Mr Caracco's landlady had suggested, and ordered that Chivvy Chase School be closed. It was too late for the news to reach the morning papers, but the whole Chivvy Chase area was alive with rumours, which soon began to spread across the country.

In Parliament the discussion about the Brain Sharpener's proposal went the usual way. When one side favoured making an agreement, the other side came out against it, and it was this which so annoyed the Brain Sharpener that he had suddenly disappeared.

For some time the debate went on without anyone noticing that he had gone. As soon as they did realise he was no longer there, most of them decided that probably he didn't exist. They all went home without deciding anything. But the Home Secretary did send a Secret Agent to go and sit by Mr Browser's bed and find out all he could as soon as possible.

The nursing staff only gave permission for Mr Browser to speak at midday the next day.

'Who are you?' he asked, when the Secret Agent sat at his bedside.

'I represent the Government,' said the Agent. 'We would like to know where you have been, and also the whereabouts of your choir.'

'Has the Government made an agreement with the Brain Sharpeners?' was Mr Browser's reply.

'That,' said the Secret Agent, 'is Top Secret information. I'm afraid I'm not able to tell you.'

'In that case,' replied Mr Browser, 'I'm afraid I can't tell you anything, except that if the Government doesn't make an agreement quickly, the choir will be gone for ever, and what's more we shall probably be taken over by the Brain Sharpeners. Nurse! Nurse! I'd like to talk to the press, please. It's time everybody knew what the Brain Sharpeners aim to do, and what needs to be done to save the choir.'

The Secret Agent looked as though he would have liked to gag Mr Browser, but the sister of the ward was standing behind the nurse, looking at her most severe.

'I think you are annoying this patient,' she said. 'Perhaps you had better leave.'

'Go and talk to Mr Sage at Chivvy Chase School,' advised Mr Browser. 'Maybe he'll be able to tell you something.'

'He can't be found,' said the Secret Agent. 'Nor can the boy who you are supposed to have said came with you.'

'He did,' said Mr Browser. 'Oh dear, poor Spiky!'

The Secret Agent left, and Mr Browser insisted that, in order to save the choir and the world, he must speak to the press and make the Government more strongly aware of the danger of delay.

He talked, and the newspapers blazoned the Brain Sharpeners all over their pages.

'BRAIN SHARPENERS KIDNAP HEAD-MASTER.'

'TEACHER JOINS CHOIR IN SPACE.'

'BRAIN SHARPENERS DEMAND – NO MORE ROCKETS.'

'NO MORE MISSILES, SAY BRAIN SHARPENERS.'

'BROWSER FORECASTS BRAIN SHARP-ENER TAKEOVER.'

The Chivvy Chase School Parents' Association was quick to act. A petition was sent to the Prime Minister demanding that an agreement be signed in order that their children should be returned.

There's no doubt that the Government was shaken by the disappearance of Mr Sage and Mr Caracco, especially after what the Brain Sharpener had told them he was capable of doing.

'We are all in danger of being kidnapped too,' said one of the Ministers. 'We certainly can't win the next election from Outer Space.'

'But how are we going to make contact now?' somebody asked.

'There's only one hope,' said the Home Secretary. 'We'd better go and talk to this Mr Browser, and see if he has any ideas.'

So Mr Browser, who by good fortune was much better after a straightforward appendicitis operation, found himself surrounded by a delegation from the Government.

'Could you possibly make contact with the Brain Sharpeners?' he was begged. 'We want to make peace with them, on their terms.'

'I'm afraid,' said Mr Browser, 'you've let your chance slip. The Brain Sharpeners make contact with us, not the other way round. By thinking hard I might alert them, if they are still keeping a watch on me, but it's doubtful. My brain hasn't been sharpened enough.'

'They've threatened to kidnap the whole Government,' Mr Browser was told. 'We just didn't believe it was possible, that's why we didn't act more quickly.'

Mr Browser was slightly worried about the possible kidnapping of the Government, but the mental takeover of the world by the Brain Sharpeners was something which had always concerned him. He thought hard.

'There's only one possibility,' he said.

'Yes?' They all leaned over his bed.

'Find out the course which the last rocket

took – the one which wandered away and alerted the Brain Sharpeners, and send another one off in the same direction. Write a signed agreement on a big sheet, and let it fly from the rocket when it's out in space.'

The Ministers discussed the proposition.

'America will have to agree,' said one. 'The rockets are fired from there.'

'We can tell them we're only doing it to get our children back,' said another.

'Is it possible to hang a message out in Space?' asked a third.

'Oh dear,' said Mr Browser, yawning. 'Such matters can surely be dealt with by our space satellite experts. One of them's bound to think he can do it. I'm really rather tired, and I'd prefer to leave all that to you, if you don't mind.'

'You'd better run along now,' said the nurse. 'He's still a little weak.'

So the Ministers ran along, and discussed Mr Browser's suggestion earnestly all the way back to London. They even argued about the wording on the sheet to be hung out in Space, but finally agreed on: 'WE HEREBY AGREE NOT TO SEND ROCKETS AND MISSILES INTO OUTER SPACE, AND TO STOP ALL MANUFACTURE OF NEW NUCLEAR WEAPONS. PLEASE SEND BACK THE CHIVVY CHASE SCHOOL

CHOIR. SIGNED, PRIME MINISTER, HOME SECRETARY, FOREIGN SECRETARY.'

'If we pull this off, and the choir returns, we'll hold an election at once,' said the Prime Minister, and the others all approved. But they all still looked very serious, because they weren't sure whether their scientists could manage to put another rocket on the same course as the previous one.

In hospital, Mr Browser lay back but did not sleep. He was thinking hard, trying to concentrate his mind in the faint hope of attracting the attention of the Brain Sharpeners. Deep down he thought he was more likely to succeed than the scientists with their rocket and message displayed in Space.

8
The District Choir Festival

In spite of the absence of the Chivvy Chase School choir, arrangements went ahead to hold the annual Choir Festival for the local schools as planned. The other schools saw no reason to cancel it, especially as Chivvy Chase had not taken part for many years. The appointed day was fine and warm, and half an hour before the start coaches arrived and the competing schools were unloaded. First came Lower Lane School, winners for the past two years. They were followed by St. Mathilda's School, each child complete in its uniform and obeying an instruction to keep a promise of silence from the time they entered the hall to the time they started singing. Then came the Kenneth Ogdon Primary School, frequent winners and confident that under the baton of Miss Pringle, L.R.A.M., they would achieve success again. Two more schools completed the number, but they were unlikely to win. The main struggle would no doubt be between Lower Lane and Kenneth Ogdon schools.

The judges arrived just as the Festival was due to start. One of them was Mr Jolyon Morten, the Inspector, another was the Education Officer for

the area, who was there chiefly because he was afraid lest another choir might vanish, and wanted to keep his eye on them all. The other judges were two ladies hiding under big hats, one of whom was a local Councillor and the other a retired Headmistress who had attended the Festival for the past forty years.

The Festival began with a one minute's silence in honour of the vanished Chivvy Chase School choir. Then one of the outsider schools began singing their three songs a little too loudly, and the judges smiled and made entries in their notebooks. St. Mathilda's came next, and sang 'Morning Has Broken' a little too softly, and followed with two almost unknown songs which were well sung but did not inspire the judges.

At this point Mr Browser, who was still convalescing, slipped into his seat at the back of the hall. The next school, which had stepped in to take the place of Chivvy Chase, forgot their words in one song and earned polite but pitying smiles from the judges. Kenneth Ogdon School put up an excellent performance – the only doubts in the judges' minds were about their third song, 'Bluebells in the Woods', which had been written by Miss Pringle, and it was easy for the judges to hear that it very much resembled another more famous song.

Finally, Lower Lane School performed admirably, and what's more sang the favourite songs of three of the judges. The children filed off the platform to ringing applause, and the judges tried not to show their satisfaction too clearly.

They were about to start working out how many marks out of a hundred each school should be given, when it seemed a kind of hurricane blew up outside the hall. Programmes and musical scores were blown about, doors banged and windows rattled like machine gun fire. The hall darkened, and there was a bright flash like sheet lightning close at hand. Judges, choirs and the audience were all blinded for a second, and many put their hands to their eyes for protection.

When they could see properly again they looked in amazement at the stage. Sitting there, ready to sing their first song, were the children of Chivvy Chase School choir. Standing alongside them were Mr Sage and Mr Caracco, the latter holding his guitar. The judges gave way to surprise, and stared open mouthed like any ordinary mortals.

'May we sing our first song?' asked Mr Sage, and the judges nodded and the hall was absolutely quiet. 'And may Mr Caracco accompany them on his guitar?' went on Mr Sage. 'He's been practising with them since Mr Browser was taken ill.'

'I'm here!' called out Mr Browser. He was allowed to come forward to conduct, and Mr Caracco also positioned himself ready to play the guitar accompaniment, to which the choir seemed used.

'Are they real?' whispered members of the audience one to another – and everyone was afraid to interrupt the choir or make a movement which might cause it to disappear again.

Spiky Jackson seemed real enough when he sneezed before announcing the first song, 'Yellow Bird'. This was followed by 'The Skye Boat Song', and finally Spiky introduced the third song.

'You may know it as "A Song for the World",' he

said, 'but we prefer to call it "The Brain Sharpeners' Song".'

As soon as it began everyone recognised it as the song sung by the choir when it appeared in London. It was sung perfectly, and the audience applauded wildly – and just a little hysterically.

'Chivvy Chase, please remain where you are while the judging takes place,' announced one of the judges. 'We weren't expecting you, so there isn't any space for you on the floor of the hall. We are, of course, delighted to have you back with us.' And she gave the choir a funny look as if she expected it to vanish at any second.

A young lady journalist who had been dozing at the back of the hall, having been sent to cover the Festival by the local paper, suddenly realised that she was in on the hottest story ever, and that if she handled things right her future was rosy. She rushed out of the hall to the nearest telephone booth, and began ringing a national newspaper, then T.V., then radio and finally her own paper.

The judges were bent over their notebooks, discussing various points with very serious expressions on their faces. They kept on looking round to see if the Chivvy Chase children were still there. They were, and they were beginning to grasp that they had really come back home. Anna Cardwell began doing a little jig, and Spiky Jackson stood on his chair with hands aloft, as though he'd just scored the winning goal in the World Cup Final.

The lady Councillor in the big hat climbed up on the platform, and Mr Sage tried to calm his choir down. The audience fell silent, and the judge began her summing up.

'Green Street School,' she began, 'sang with great heart and showed much promise for the future, especially as they haven't been here very often. We award them 80 marks out of 100. St. Mathilda's sang with much feeling – a very pleasing performance. 81 marks. David Livingstone School did very well in spite of forgetting the words, and they have 83 marks. The Kenneth Ogdon School sang beautifully. We thought them very brave to try a brand new song' – a glance at Miss Pringle – 'and we give them a well deserved 86 marks. We would all like to congratulate Lower Lane School on the standard of their singing and their choice of songs. They receive 89 marks, one of the highest marks we have ever given. Finally, what a pleasant surprise to see Chivvy Chase School here. We must congratulate them on overcoming all their difficulties and singing delightfully, especially their last song, which I am sure moved us all tremendously. To Chivvy Chase School we award 89½ marks, and I therefore ask their Headmaster

Mr Sage to come forward and accept the Festival Shield for the coming year!'

The announcement of their victory confirmed to the Chivvy Chase children that they were back in the world, and they stood up and cheered and waved their arms. Mr Sage and Mr Caracco were welcomed by Mr Browser, and the judges came across to congratulate them. A parent of a Lower Lane child who was very friendly with Spiky Jackson's father, slipped out of the hall and made a telephone call.

'Stay here, children,' said the Education Officer, 'and we will contact your parents through the Parents' Association. I'll go and phone them now.'

'Thank goodness you're back,' said Mr Browser to Mr Sage. 'So the Government must have been in contact with the Brain Sharpeners somehow. I tried very hard.'

'We weren't told very much,' said Mr Sage, 'except that we were to be sent back. I think they began to despair of us ever being able to sing properly in Russian, and decided they'd have to try some other way.'

All conversation ceased when the door at the back of the hall burst open.

'They're back!' cried Spiky Jackson's father.

'Anna! Whatever have you been up to?' demanded Mrs Cardwell. The news from the Lower

Lane parent had spread around, and parents were soon streaming into the hall.

Great were the rejoicings on the platform as parents grabbed their children and were delighted to find that they were solid. Mr Sage and Mr Browser were forgiven, and Mr Caracco was praised for agreeing to go up into Space to take Mr Browser's place. Then they all went home to eat a solid meal.

'I'm fed up with the pills the Brain Sharpeners gave us,' declared Spiky. 'I hope they never take over down here, even though they're so clever.'

That, of course, will be up to the world's leaders. Whether the Brain Sharpeners have started to work on the world's most powerful nations is not yet clear; sometimes it looks like it, when the leaders talk about cutting down the number of bombs and missiles.

'Let's hope something is really done,' said Spiky Jackson, 'because I don't want to live on pills for the rest of my life under the rule of the Brain Sharpeners.'

'Even that,' declared the serious Selwyn Jordan, 'would be better than being blown up by bombs made by our own race.' And Spiky agreed.

Anna Cardwell was just glad to be back, but she did make one comment on the Brain Sharpeners when Mr Sage showed the Festival Shield proudly

to the whole school.

'I think,' she whispered, 'that the judges were under the influence of the Brain Sharpeners when they made us come first. The Brain Sharpeners just couldn't bear not to win.'

Fortunately Mr Sage couldn't hear her, and if Mr Browser did, he pretended to take no notice.

On the following pages you will find some other exciting Beaver Books to look out for in your local bookshop